What the Tide Brings

HEATHER EWINGS

Quamby Press

What the Tide Brings
First Published 22 April 2020

Quamby Press
QuambyPress@outlook.com.au

ISBN: 978-0-6488124-1-8

Cover image: Free-Photos from Pixabay

A catalogue record for this work is available from the National Library of Australia

To Kynan,

for all your love and support that got me here. xx

Prologue

Alfred untied the clinker, pushing it across the sandy beach until it bobbed in the waves. As the water reached his shins he threw the rope in, climbing after it and taking hold of the oars.

In no time, he'd moved beyond the breakers, and with only a few more strokes familiar faces bobbed above the waves; long whiskers on trembling noses, enormous dark eyes that always looked on the verge of tears despite the creatures' joyful high-pitched barks.

"Ready for another day?" Alfred asked.

They responded by rolling and twisting in the water, their joyful chattering almost blocking the wash of waves upon the shore.

"Let's go."

The creatures slipped beneath the waves, leaving only the sound of oars slapping the water, and seagulls calling overhead.

Alfred relaxed into a steady pace, watching the beach recede and then vanish as his boat travelled around the point. The coast was an array of colour, the last of the yellow of coltsfoot and celandine mingling with the fresh red and pink of thrift, campion and orchids. Above it all, wisps of cloud streaked a pale sky, and below it the sea was dark and deep.

A distant splash woke Alfred out of his reverie and he drew in the oars, stowing them safely along either side of the boat. He lifted the net, and at the signal from another splash, cast it out.

The sea rippled as a school of fish headed straight for his trap, the salt water churning as they fought to be free of the net. Alfred hauled it in, allowing the catch to spill open in his boat. He scoured through the pile, tossing the good-sized fish into a small wooden cask half-filled with sea water, and throwing the too-small fish back into the sea.

"Done well." Alfred flipped the biggest of the fish to the seals now floating on their backs around his boat, clapping their flippers in celebration of their effort.

"That's enough for today."

In the past, Alfred would have stayed on to bring in two or three chests full of fish. But time had passed since he was a lone fisherman fishing for the entire village, and now he needed only enough to feed himself and to barter with others.

He sat for a moment, watching the seals frolic, not yet ready to return to solid ground.

"Tis almost a shame I can't join you." He lifted the oars, slotting them back into the thole. "Except I think I'd rather be on the sea, than in it. Anyway. Can't be sittin' out here all day, not when there's work to be done."

The seals swam alongside his boat on the return journey, leaping and chattering. All but one slipped beneath the waves before Alfred drew in line with the farthest point of the rocky outcrop.

"You coming ashore later, Oulde?"

A single bark gave him his answer.

"Dusk?"

A nod and a splash and she was gone.

Alfred pulled the boat well above the high tide line, secured it to a tree and hauled his catch out onto the sand and back along the path to his hut. Here, he cleaned his fish; gutting and scaling - keeping the waste to bury in his garden to fertilise his vegetables. He packed the fillets in salt and hauled the cask up onto his back for the three mile walk into town.

∞

It was dark as Alfred made his way back to the shore, back aching from an afternoon's woodcutting, stomach satisfied with his supper of fried fish and buttery mashed potatoes from his garden.

A sharp bark alerted him to Oulde's presence.

"I know, I know, running late as usual." He dropped the pack from his shoulder and removed an oversized woollen cardigan. He squeezed his eyes shut as he held it between outstretched arms. In moments an arm slipped into one sleeve and then the other, and he opened his eyes.

"You can look, you know." Oulde smiled at

him, wisps of grey hair tickling the laugh lines around her eyes.

"I was taught it was rude to watch a lady undress." Alfred leaned in close and kissed her cheek.

"Still, after all this time…."

Alfred rummaged around in his pack, pulling out the hunk of goats' cheese and bread, and the flasks; fresh water for her, whisky for himself.

Oulde took the blanket and spread it out on the sand, helping Alfred to sit.

"These old bones are seizing up on me, Oulde. Won't be long'n I'll have to move closer to the village—find someone younger to help care for me."

"Oh hush! You've years in you yet." Oulde accepted the flask of water.

"Tis your fish keeping me young," he said, holding his own flask up to tap against Oulde's for a 'cheers'. "How are things with the colony?"

Oulde sighed.

"Wayanna's grown into quite the rebel. Such a stubborn streak; she always wants to be on the beach. Wants to find her parents, she says. Wants to bring her mother back."

Alfred lay back on the sand to look at the stars.

"What do you tell her?"

Oulde shrugged. "What can I say? We haven't spoken to her mother since her birth. How can we? The girl needs to give up on this foolish notion." Oulde shook her head. "You know I long for her mother's return, but if the woman doesn't know her heritage, how can she come back to it?"

Alfred nodded. "If she was going to return, it would have been when Dyllis died. She didn't."

"And the old man?"

Alfred shook his head. "Duncan doesn't know."

Oulde sighed. "It's too long to hold onto such pain." Her voice cracked. Alfred shifted closer and wrapped an arm around his dearest friend.

"What's done is done. Ain't no changing the past, only making the best of what the tide brings."

Part 1

Chapter 1

Myna dreamed.

Stars spilled along the Milky Way and Myna nearly stumbled on the path for gazing at them instead of watching her feet.

Why am I out so late?

She stopped, brow furrowed as she fought to recall the reason for her night-time stroll, and then a soft swell of sound broke over the waves, a hum, a call, and she remembered that *this* was why she was out, to follow the song, to see who made it, and why.

The path led over the dunes, furrowed out by thousands of feet over thousands of years, and as

Myna reached the crest the moon rose above the horizon, full and bright, lighting up the silvery-white curve of the beach below and leaving a path of dancing light across the ocean.

There was little to see from here. The sand reflected the moonlight, revealing no movement on the beach, but farther around the bay at the point all was in shadow.

Still the sound crescendoed, eerie and sweet over the gentle wash of the waves.

Myna followed the sound down the path and along the shore. As she approached the point, movement caught her eye, a tall shadow rising above the rocks that tumbled from the point into the sea.

Myna hesitated, suddenly aware of how clear she must be to whoever sang, her form stark against the white sand. But the shadow didn't move, and as she crept nearer she realised the figure looked away, out over the ocean beyond the point.

Myna stepped up onto the rocks, drawn by the cover the dark rocks would give her, her eyes fixed on the shadow, only a few metres away now. A loose stone wobbled underfoot, knocking against the next in a moment of breath between verses, and Myna sucked in a breath.

The shadow turned.

'Sorry.' Myna spread her arms for balance, her gaze on her feet as she found a sturdier rock. 'I didn't mean to disturb you.' *What am I doing here?*

The shadow took a step closer and Myna glanced up to see a girl of about sixteen, whose face she knew.

'Mother!' the young woman exclaimed. 'You came. I knew you would come.' She beamed, and Myna felt a rush of joy as the girl stepped down to embrace her.

'Of course I came.' She shook her head. How silly to forget her daughter liked to come to the shore to sing. 'But it's late. Time to come home now.'

'Just a little longer, Mother. I do so love the sea air.'

Myna's heart swelled as she watched her daughter turn and climb the rocks again, those eerie-sweet sounds filling the night with such precious music.

A golden light shone behind Myna, and she turned, opening her eyes. Sunlight filtering through the shutters blinded her for a moment and she blinked to clear her vision. Ronan, her husband, slept beside her, his mouth slightly agape with soft snores.

Myna wrapped her arms around her swelling stomach and smiled.

'You're a daughter, are you? With the most beautiful voice.' Her stomach stretched, a lump pushing up underneath her arm and sliding across her belly to disappear again on the other side, and she rubbed the spot. 'Was that a yes? Well then, we'll have to think of a good name for you.'

Chapter 2

Myna rubbed her swollen belly, pushing back against the limb fighting for space inside.

'Not long now, little one. Soon you'll be able to stretch those legs as much as you want.'

There was a bittersweet tang at the thought of it; the excitement of meeting her child for the first time, and yet the loss of this precious time when it was just Myna and her infant, when interactions involved movement and stretches and pushing from within, and rubbing and stroking and talking from without.

Could she look after a child on the outside, as well as her body managed while it was inside? And what if something went wrong? She'd never experienced such joy in her life; what made her worthy of it now?

∞

Myna had been rolling with the contractions for hours. She gripped Ronan's hand as another wave surged through her body.

'You're fully dilated, not long now.' Oulde, the midwife, spoke in soothing tones as she withdrew her fingers from between Myna's legs. With Ronan's help, she brought Myna back to a standing position.

Myna cringed as the contraction coursed through her body. 'I'm not sure I can walk anymore.' She spoke through gasps, between ever strengthening waves that crippled her.

'Just a little longer, love. It'll be over in a moment,' Ronan murmured.

Earlier in the night, Myna had snapped at him for such ridiculous comments. As if he knew the first thing about birthing a child! But now her energy was fading. Summoning the will to stand, to walk, took every ounce of her strength.

They paced the room. Back and forth, back

and forth, Myna's arm across Ronan's shoulders, his arm across her back, holding her up. With each new wave that rose and crested Myna tensed, and Ronan stood, holding her up as her fingers dug into his flesh.

It was taking too long.

The pain changed, and Myna's knees collapsed underneath her, the desire to bear down overtaking everything else.

'That's it,' Oulde cooed. 'That's a girl, good work, keep it up.'

Ronan took up the mantra. 'That's the way, not long now.'

Myna leaned forward so her arms could bear some of the weight of her oversized body. She gave in to the urge to push, letting out a deep groan as the baby moved lower.

'We can see the head,' Oulde said. 'Take it slow now, easy does it.'

Those words provided the burst of energy Myna needed.

'Another push now, all right, ease off, take a breath. Now one more.'

Pressure built between Myna's legs, her skin pulled so tight she thought she must tear, then released, just a little, as a gush of water spilled out onto the floor.

'Oh!' Oulde jerked a hand back as though she'd been burned.

Myna tried to peer around. 'What's wrong?'

A pause. Then Oulde spoke. 'Nothing, Myna. Everything's fine. Now come on, we need you to give another big push, let's get this body out.'

Myna called up on all her reserves, fighting the stab of fear in her chest. With one almighty push she felt the baby slither out from between her legs.

Silence.

Where was the baby's cry?

'Is everything all right?' She tried to turn but Oulde put a hand on her back.

'We have to cut the cord now. You just stay there.'

The knife flashed in the candle light, pulling against the cord, still attached to something inside her.

Myna's chest constricted. Why were they all so quiet?

'We'll just wrap the baby now, and get you comfy so you can deliver the placenta.'

In moments Oulde was helping Myna sit, but then she heard the thud of the door.

'Where's Ronan and the baby? Do we have a daughter?'

Contractions racked her body again, and Myna bore down as Oulde gently pulled on umbilical cord.

'Come on, now. Not much longer.'

'I just want to see my baby.' Myna spoke through gritted teeth, fighting back the tears that pricked at her eyes.

One final push and a fleshy red mess landed on the cloth beneath her.

Oulde wrapped it, carefully wiping between Myna's legs with a warm damp cloth.

'Let me see her.'

'Shh, now. Let's just get you onto the bed.' Oulde gripped under Myna's arm, helping her to stand.

Myna fought back the fear rising in her chest. 'What's wrong? What's happened?'

'Don't worry yourself, Myna, dear.' Oulde pulled the blankets up around Myna's waist. She left the room for a moment, returning with a mug of something warm.

'Drink this. It'll help.'

Myna did as she was told.

'You just rest. Ronan will be back soon.'

Myna sank bank into the pillows. Her body had never felt so heavy.

Oulde left the room, and Myna allowed her eyelids to close.

She couldn't even rouse herself when Ronan's panicked whisper drifted through the closed door.

'What do we do?'

℘

A wave of revulsion passed through Ronan's body as he looked on the infant his wife had just birthed. He didn't want to touch it, but when he put it down a strange slit opened where the mouth should be, and a strange mewling sound emerged, so he picked it up as he paced the room, waiting for Oulde.

The door opened and closed, and he turned.

'What do we do?' His heart pounded in his ears.

'There's nothing we can do.' Oulde was calm;

brisk and business-like. 'I'll deal with it; you don't need to worry about a thing.'

'What?'

'You can't raise it—look at it.'

'It'll break Myna's heart.'

'Even more so if she sees it. Best you let it go. We'll tell her it died. She doesn't need to see *that*.'

Ronan looked down at the creature in his arms. The grey tinged skin was nothing compared with the large black eyes without even a hint of white, and two slits where the nose should be. It seemed to be covered by some sort of translucent skin, holding the arms and legs tight against the body, preventing movement.

There was a sense in Oulde's words, and Ronan felt only relief as he passed the baby over. It was for the best. Myna had suffered through enough in her life. To see she'd given birth to something so… monstrous…would break her.

But then Oulde was gone, and Ronan's arms were empty, their longed-for addition to the family no more.

Chapter 3

'Come on, love. It's a beautiful day. Won't you come out? I've made you a cup of tea. We could sit together. Soak up some sunshine and fresh air.'

Myna opened her bleary eyes. She blinked once, and buried her face in the pillow, pulling the blanket above her head.

Ronan wasn't even sure she'd seen him.

It had been months now since he'd handed the baby over to the midwife to deal with; months since he'd felt the heart-wrenching emptiness in his arms as he realised that the baby they'd so longed for was gone.

He'd returned to the room to find Myna sleeping. Oulde had given her a tonic to help her

rest while he and Oulde cleaned the room,
removing all trace of the birth, anything that might
remind Myna of what she'd been through.

'It'll take some time,' Oulde had said. 'But if
you don't speak of it, she'll forget soon enough.
Then things can go back to the way they were. No
use pining over things that weren't meant to be.'

Ronan had nodded. He remembered that he'd
nodded, taken her words to heart, trusted that she
knew best.

But spring had turned to summer had turned
to autumn, and Myna still cried herself to sleep
every night, and hid herself from the world every
day. Ronan went through the motions: cooking,
cleaning, gardening. Every morning he hoped for
improvement and every morning Myna's sorrowful
eyes tore holes in his heart.

He set the tea on the low table on Myna's side
of the bed.

In the kitchen he drank his own tea, ate the
bland oats that served as breakfast and hauled the
case onto his back. The trip into town wasn't long,
but it was arduous. A steep slippery descent was
the path to the village, the scree apt to jump free
under your feet and send you hurtling down the cliff

face to the jagged rock below.

It took sturdy boots, a sure foot, and the blessings of the gods to ensure a safe descent, and even then there might still be a scrape or scratch, or even a twisted ankle.

Today it seemed the gods smiled at him, or else they thought his wife's misery enough punishment for the heavy weight of guilt he carried. Their baby had lived, after all. It had not died at birth as he and Oulde had told Myna. Perhaps they *should* have shown her the child—let her see why it could not live—before taking it away. Perhaps Myna would have felt the revulsion he'd felt and would no longer be mourning the daughter who still visited her dreams.

Ronan shook his head. If he felt guilt and revulsion both, then she would have felt that triple-fold. She'd probably have insisted on keeping it, and then where would they be? An image came to mind of the deformed torso, the arms moulded to the body, the legs fused together. He shuddered. No. It was better she hadn't seen it. Better than face the horror that had grown inside her.

'Ronan.'

He looked up. 'Alfred.'

'Myna still not improved?'

Ronan shook his head, blinking away the tears blurring his vision.

'Take this.' Alfred held out a large fish by the gills.

'We can't take that—'

Alfred held up a hand. 'I blame meself. I should've said something a long time ago.'

Ronan frowned. 'Sorry?'

Alfred shook his head. 'The fish, lad. I should've had someone bring the fish, when me leg gave out. Maybe she wouldn't be suffering as she is. Maybe—' He shook his head again. 'That wife of yours has been an important part of my life. You take this. There's good oils in fish. They'll help her get better.' Alfred's voice was gruff. 'Besides, the fish have returned to the bay. The fishin's good again. I'm catching too much to manage myself.'

Ronan took the fish. 'Thank you, Alfred.'

Alfred kept a hold until Ronan caught his eye.

'You come and get a fish from me anytime you come into the village. I can't get up that hill no more, but you come see me, and I'll give you a fish. Anything to see that girl back on her feet.'

'Thank you, Alfred. That means a lot.'

'Just make sure you do it, lad. She needs to get better. Losing a child's a terrible thing, but we can't have her joining it.'

Ronan swallowed back the lump that formed in his throat. 'No. No, we can't.'

Chapter 4

Ronan held his breath as Myna lifted a portion of fish with her fork. She brought it to her mouth, chewed, swallowed, and picked up another portion.

If Myna had been herself she would've asked where the money came from for such a meal. Or perhaps she would have guessed.

All Ronan wanted was for her to speak to him again.

'Alfred gave me the fish.'

She glanced up from her plate. Her eyes were puffy, her hair tousled. She took a bite, chewed and swallowed. She picked up another piece with her fork, considered it a moment, and put that piece into her mouth too.

'He said he'd give me a fish every time I went into town. He said you were very important to him, that it was important you got better.' Ronan fought to keep his voice from breaking.

Myna frowned. 'Alfred?'

Ronan nodded. 'Alfred said you were important to him,' he repeated.

'Alfred was one of Father's friends, a long time ago. He used to bring us fish every day when I was a child.'

'He brought you fish every day? Why?' Ronan already knew this story, but now Myna had started to speak he needed her to continue.

Myna shrugged. 'Before I was born, they say that ours was the busiest fishing port in the whole district. But then the fish vanished. Alfred was the only one who could still catch any. I guess he brought them over because he and Father were friends.'

Ronan put down his fork. 'I never knew Alfred and your father had been close.'

Myna shrugged again. 'He and Father had a falling out, I suppose.'

'Over what? Your father seems pretty vocal of his dislike of people, but he's never said anything of

Alfred.'

'How should I know, Ronan!' Myna narrowed her eyes, and pushed her plate away. 'I'm not my father's keeper. What does it matter, anyway? Maybe Alfred's just a creepy old man with no children of his own.'

She stormed off to the bedroom, and Ronan heard the creak of their bed as she threw herself on it.

As he cleared the table he couldn't help allowing a little burst of hope. She'd eaten at least half of her meal, where she normally pushed it aside after a bite or two. She'd spoken to him, in full sentences. And she'd allowed herself to get angry. It was progress, he decided. She'd cracked the ice, just a little. He hoped it might not take too much more to shatter it completely.

ૹ

'If you'd let me in, I could've helped. I know all the charms to help protect the pregnant mother and her baby. I could've done something.'

Dyllis bustled around the kitchen, wiping crumbs off the table into her hand.

'You brought this on yourself, the two of you. You especially—staying during a childbirth! It's a woman's space, that is. There's no place for men at a birthing. And then to invite in a stranger—who knows what the woman did. I've lived in these parts my whole life and I've never heard of an 'Oulde' before. She probably cursed you both.'

Ronan stood by the bedroom door, arms crossed across his chest. He wished he could expand his body so it filled the space and prevented any sound from passing through. Myna had suffered enough already, and yet this woman would not give up, reciting her lecture every time she visited. The best Ronan could do was stop her from barging in on Myna and causing more distress.

'Myna was a gift. I tried so hard to have a child, and I couldn't, for so long, and then the Sea heard my plea for a baby and delivered Myna to me. And now you've stolen my chance at a grandchild. The two of you. If I'd been here—'

'Myna would never have coped had you been here. The labour probably would've taken her as well.' Ronan spoke through gritted teeth, words he'd long bottled up.

Dyllis looked up in surprise.

'Well, I never! After all we've done for you. You came to this town with nothing, and we built you a house, on our land—'

'Alfred contributed half the house, for the work I'd done for him. And this land isn't yours—it belongs to no one. It's the place no one wants to live because it's so far away from anything. You're here because you were cast out from the village. Don't think I don't know that story.'

Dyllis sucked in a breath, jutting out her chin and straightening her shoulders. 'You don't know half the story! If you think you're better than us, simply because of a misunderstanding in our past, then you can just move back into that village. I can take care of my daughter myself.'

Ronan almost laughed. 'Your daughter doesn't want to be taken care of by you. You don't *care*; you harass, you intimidate, you get under her and everybody else's skin.'

'Then why didn't she move away when she had the chance? Why would she insist you build your home here, so close to us?'

Ronan narrowed his eyes. It felt so good to be giving voice to everything he'd held inside. 'She doesn't believe she has a place in the village. Whatever it was you did in the past, it made her an outcast, too.'

'You have no idea what we've been through as a family.' She spat the words at him. 'And you never will.'

Dyllis strode out the door, allowing it to bang shut behind her, and Ronan sank against the wall, his heart pounding. But then Myna's soft sobs carried to him through the walls and the relief flooding his system at saying words long locked away passed, regret taking its place. He should've kept quiet. Myna already suffered enough. She didn't need her husband and mother fighting.

Chapter 5

Myna's earliest memories were her happiest. Tending the garden with Mother, snaring with Father, swinging high on the plank her parents had hung from a branch of the great old oak—the breeze whistling past her ears.

She remembered Alfred's visits—a ruffling of her hair in greeting, occasionally a treat, and always a fish; the largest and tastiest of his catch.

She'd not known the ocean existed, then.

She discovered it on her first trip to town. She'd felt like such a grown-up girl, accompanying Father down the slippery scree, making their way through the woods to follow the path to the town.

But then she saw it—that great expanse of

blue, deeper than the sky and sparkling like the creek that gurgled its way across the meadow. The ocean called to her with such strength she dropped the parcel she'd begged Father to let her carry, spilling pods of peas and ears of corn across the path, and raced towards the blue. The powdery sand gave her pause, but only for a moment and she was off again, knee-deep in water before she heard Father's desperate calls.

She turned just as he reached her, yanking her back by her arm, out of the sea, and back across the beach.

'Are you crazy? Your mother will be furious!'

Myna remembered frowning. 'Why?'

Father had paused, his mouth opening and closing. Then, 'Look at your trousers!'

She'd glanced down. Cut off just below the knee, it was only the cuffs that were wet, and she'd laughed. She'd never seen her mother angry. Myna played in the creek all the time, and Mother was never angry about wet clothes, not even when she fell in and was drenched from head to toe. She helped Father pick up the scattered vegetables, and they continued to market.

But Myna couldn't concentrate on the stall.

Even from where they stood in the village green she could hear the waves; the crash as they struck the shore, the whoosh as they returned to sea.

She stole away while her father was deep in conversation, down to the shore between two houses. She removed her sandals high up on the beach and picked her way across the stones, dipping her foot into the icy swell.

Her toe tingled. In moments, Myna had stripped off all her clothes and waded out to where it was deep enough to dive in.

She ventured farther and farther out, diving deeper each time, as deep as her lungs would allow her to go and even then holding on fit to burst, just for that time under the water.

She hadn't realised they'd been looking for her. She hadn't heard their calls, never had a thought for those on land until two strong hands pulled her from the water and into a boat.

When they realised she wasn't drowning they took away the blanket—punishment for one who caused such panic. And then came the beating. Her doting mother hit her with a wooden spoon, enough lashes across her bottom and legs that she couldn't sit properly for days.

Chapter 6

Ronan stood at the bedroom door.

'I fell in love with you on sight.' He watched
the pile of blankets that hid his wife. 'I saw you on
the beach that day, sitting alone, your gaze focused
on the sea, and even from that distance I could feel
how sad you were. All I wanted to do was make you
happy.'

Myna gave no response.

'When you agreed to marry me, well, I think
that was the happiest day of my life,' he continued.
'And there was light in your eyes, and I thought
maybe it was the happiest day of yours, too. And
then you told me we were having a child, and I felt

the movement in your belly, and I know I've never felt such joy as I felt then, with that promise of life to come. You *bloomed* for all those months. You were so radiant. In all my life I never imagined I'd be lucky enough to experience such wonder.'

A muffled sob emerged from the beneath the bedclothes.

'When the midwife bundled our little one in a blanket and passed it to me, I—' Ronan stopped. He had been going to say how perfect their infant was, but he couldn't lie. He took a deep breath and moved across to the bed, resting a hand on the pile where he guessed Myna's shoulder might be.

'Our child wasn't well, Myna. Its face and body were…squashed.' He couldn't bring himself to admit it had been alive. 'I didn't know what to do. Oulde said it would be best if you didn't see. She said it would be hard enough…but to see it...' He stopped, fighting the catch in his throat. Under the blankets, Myna stirred.

'I did it for you, Myna. I didn't want you to see...that. But after she took it, I…I felt such an emptiness. Our dreams of the future, gone. But most of all, your happiness, torn away. I'd give anything to see you smile again, love. I've missed you, so much.'

As he spoke Myna pushed the covers back, and her puffy face peered up at him.

'What was it?'

'What was what?' Ronan frowned.

'The baby! Did we have a son or a daughter? You keep saying 'it', why not 'he' or 'she'?'

'Oh.' Ronan had been so shocked by the baby's face he hadn't thought to check its gender. Then he thought of the legs, fused together. 'It was a girl. We had a daughter.'

Myna's head fell back into the pillow. 'Ebba,' she whispered.

'Ebba?'

Myna bit her lip. 'It's the name I picked out for a daughter.' She looked up at him. 'Can we build her a cairn? Somewhere I can visit, and place some flowers? Can we stop pretending she never existed?'

Ronan nodded, so grateful to hear Myna speak, to have her look at him.

'We can,' he said. 'Do you want to come outside? You can select a place.'

Myna nodded, and Ronan helped her out of bed, and out into the sunshine.

Chapter 7

Ronan rejected Oulde's advice not to speak of the baby, fighting his own instinct to keep quiet, and gradually Myna's grief subsided.

She visited the cairn daily, in rain and mist and sunshine. She left flowers or small gifts; handwoven bracelets and necklaces, tiny cloth dolls she'd made herself. She never ventured beyond the gate of their home, but Ronan could see that the sunshine and fresh air and Alfred's fish all helped no end, and his heart soared with relief as everyday a little more colour returned to her cheeks, and her face lost that sunken look.

The years passed, and the grief softened.

Dyllis died, and Ronan was scared he'd lose his wife again. But the loss of her mother seemed more a weight lifted, and Myna continued to improve.

When she told Ronan she'd stopped taking the herbs that prevented pregnancy, his heart tore in half with the joy and the fear of it.

Part 2

Chapter 8

Ebba sighed, stretched and began to squirm.

'Shush now.' Myna was at the crib before the cry came, taking the child back to sit, and helping her to find a breast.

She eased back into the chair, her heart swelling at the contented snuffles and slurps of a baby feeding. A healthy, *living* baby.

It had been ten years since Myna's first pregnancy. Ten years since that first Ebba had died, and now she had a living child on which to bestow the name she'd loved so much. And so much had happened in those ten years; fish had returned to the bay, the village had grown again.

The haul became too much for Alfred, and then too much for Alfred and his help. Young men who'd never been to sea joined fathers whose boats sat decayed and half buried in the sand, and boat by boat the village returned to its former state.

And as fish returned to the bay, people returned to the village.

The closed expressions on the faces of the townsfolk seemed to open up, welcoming Myna in a way she'd never felt before, and with Ronan's encouragement they took a new home at the edge of the village. And not long after, Myna discovered, once again, she was pregnant.

Despite the change in fortune of all those around her, Myna still harboured fears about her pregnancy, nightmares of still-empty arms after another nine months of movement and response.

She'd made Ronan and the midwife—a different woman this time—promise to let her hold this child, no matter the outcome. Ronan had been quick to agree, and helpful in convincing the midwife despite her misgivings.

But all had gone well; an easy birth, a healthy baby, exhausted but overjoyed parents.

And as the months passed Ebba had

continued to grow as she should, into the chubby
and cheerful infant who stitched together the pieces
of Myna's heart.

Chapter 9

Myna scooped up the dirty washing from the floor of her father's bedroom, turning her face in an attempt to avoid breathing in the musty dustiness of the bundle in her arms.

'You won't find it.' Duncan tottered in the doorway, gnarled knuckles clutching the handle of his walking stick.

After her mother's death he'd had a surge of life, but now he was no longer taking care of himself and his health was deteriorating, his mind fastest of all.

Myna had learned to ignore him. Whatever was happening in his mind, it had no relevance she could see on the real world.

'You think you can fool an old man,' he continued. 'You think I don't know what you're up to, but I do. I know.' He lifted his walking stick off the floor and pointed it at her.

'Come on, Father.' Myna held the washing under one arm as she pushed gently on the end of his stick, taking a step past it to guide him back through to the kitchen and his cooling cup of tea.

'I'm just cleaning for you,' she reminded him, as she did every visit now.

'Just cleaning? And what cleaning do you need to do in the bedroom?'

'Your mattress needs turning, for a start. And the blanket needs airing. And there's the clothes you pile on the floor, and the dust on the tallboy.'

'Ha! Your mother does all those jobs for me. You wait till she gets back from town. I'll tell her you're searching for it. You'll get a beating, just like you did when you were a child. That'll teach you. All we've done for you over the years, and how do you repay us? Trying to run back to *them*, who weren't even able to look after you as a baby.'

'Ma died.' Myna put a hand on her father's shoulder. 'Almost two years ago now. She's not coming back.'

But he wasn't listening, stuck as he was in his own version of reality. 'You won't find it. Your mother hid it too well. Even I can't find it, and don't think I haven't searched long and hard.'

Myna sighed and returned to the bedroom, leaving him to ramble to himself. He'd been getting worse these past few weeks, and Myna feared he wouldn't be able to live by himself for much longer. She dreaded the thought of having him in the house with her and Ronan and little Ebba.

Chapter 10

It was dark when Myna woke. Moonbeams sneaked through gaps in the shutters, stretching the shadows in the room. Outside, waves whooshed as they washed over the sand, the sound almost reversing as they were sucked back out to sea.

She'd had that nightmare again; the young girl with dark hair, the eerie-sweet song on her lips. Once it had given her hope for the child to come, but that child had long since entered the world, been declared dead, and taken before Myna had even seen her. *Perhaps if I'd held her one time—*

Before the thought was complete a familiar eerie-sweet tune stole through the window.

Myna's heart pounded in her ears. *Not while I'm awake.* She shook her head, her hands clenching the blankets. *It's something else. It's got to be.*

She slipped out of bed, pulled on a thick woollen jumper and stole outside. The sound was stronger, clearer, but though it still sounded of the music from her dreams, Myna was convinced that up close it would fade and change, that her ears could not hear properly over the wash of the waves.

It took a few minutes to reach the shore. At first the beach looked empty. Myna stepped out, glancing first to the left, along the great stretch of sand, and then to the right, where the land curved out to the point.

At first there was nothing, but then the shadows moved and something emerged from the rocks, something with pale skin, and long dark hair teased by the wind, something which seemed to be the source of this eerie-sweet sound.

Myna shook her head. She wanted to wake up to the warmth of her bed and the safety of Ronan's strong arms, but the chill night air clung to her face and raised goosebumps on her arms.

The singing stopped.

'Mama, you came!' The figure came closer. A young woman, maybe fifteen years old.

She was naked.

'Aren't you cold?' Myna scanned the beach for clothing.

The girl laughed. 'Why would I be cold, Ma?'

Myna shook her head. 'I'm not your mother.

'You are. I'm your firstborn. They call me Wayanna, now.'

'Wayanna?' Myna frowned, shook her head. 'My firstborn died.'

The girl stepped closer. 'I'm not dead. Grandmother saved me. I was born with my skin, see.'

The girl pulled at Myna, pointing at something on the sand. Myna pulled back, refusing to budge.

The girl frowned. 'You don't know.' She looked out to sea, and then back at Myna.

'They said you didn't know.' She pulled at Myna again. This time, Myna was too cold to resist and she stumbled across the sand on numb legs. 'But you must remember being under the waves. I remember my first days, even when I was a pup. That first shock of the cold water…' Her head tilted to one side as she examined Myna. 'You don't remember, do you? You're a selkie, Mama. The human woman stole you away when you were a baby. When I was born I looked like a selkie child, and Grandmother took me to raise me in the sea.' They approached the shape in the sand and the girl lifted it up, and passed it to Myna. It was heavy; thick and rubbery, damp and warm. Myna shuddered with revulsion at the touch, but the girl didn't seem to notice. 'That's my seal skin, Mama. You have one too. The human will have hidden it somewhere. If you find it, you can come home.'

Chapter 11

Myna tossed and turned on the rickety bed as recent conversations circled her mind.

There was Wayanna's hopeful plea: 'That's my seal skin. You have one too,' quickly followed by Father's defensive tone: 'You'll never find it. Your ma hid it too well, even from me!'

Could it be true?

Myna wanted her walk to the beach to be a dream, but it hadn't ended suddenly, as dreams always did. Instead she'd had to walk the long cold path back home, and undress again, and climb back into bed beside her still sleeping husband. And then she'd lain there, for an awfully long time, as thoughts whirled around inside her head.

When the faint light of dawn crept in between the shutters, Myna sighed and slipped out of bed.

In the main room she stoked the fire, setting the kettle to boil before starting on the oats.

Father slept on a cot by the wall. Ronan intended to build an extra room for him, one that would be Ebba's once he'd passed, but though the foundation stones had been laid the walls hadn't been started, and Myna felt a stab of irritation. *How long can it take?*

As though he'd heard her thoughts, Ronan exited the bedroom, crossing the room to give Myna a kiss before leaving the house to start the morning's chores.

Myna carried the heavy pot, hanging it on the hook over the fire when she heard the cot creak.

'What am I doing here?' Father propped himself up on one elbow, blinking at her.

'You live with us now, Father.' Myna turned to remove the tea cups from the shelf and place them on the table.

'Nonsense. Take me home. Your mother will be wondering where I am.'

'Mother died years ago.'

Father sat up, swinging his legs over the side

of the bed in a rare moment of agility. 'You're trying to find it, aren't you? She'll spank you when she finds out.'

Myna lost her patience. 'My mother. Really? You've been full of tales these past months. Accusing me of searching for something I never knew existed. I thought you'd gone mad—that you suffered the derangement of old age. But you haven't, have you? You've just lost the ability to hide the truth. So, tell me about this thing I'm supposed to be looking for, that my so-called *mother* doesn't want me to find.'

He frowned, and blinked, his eyes gaining a clarity Myna hadn't seen in such a long time.

'Oh Myna.' His shoulders sagged. 'I told your mother to leave you there.'

No question how Myna found out, not even a hesitation.

'I told her it were no good, taking you from the sea. And look where it got us, a fishing village with no fish, and your mother and me ostracised, and all because of you.' His finger pointed at her, and his voice filled the room. 'But she wouldn't ever give you back, no matter how we begged and cajoled, she just wouldn't let you go.'

He sighed, his arm dropping to his lap. When he spoke again his voice was softer.

'I'm sorry, Myna, love. We were going to tell you. We just…it's hard to know when the right time falls for such talk. At every point we feared destroying your present happiness or upsetting you more than you were. Your mother struggled to conceive a child; you know that. And when she saw you…' He sighed again.

'She thought I was a gift from the sea.'

He nodded.

'So you just found me, abandoned on the beach?' Myna wanted it to be true, that the people who'd raised her had saved her, but when Duncan's gaze dropped to the table between them her hopes sank.

'You were there with a selkie woman.' His gaze flicked to Myna's face and back to the table. 'Your mother, Dyllis, she asked to hold you. The selkie was unsure, but agreed. Then Dyllis ran." Duncan's eyes flicked again. 'Selkies aren't used to running, are they? She couldn't catch up. And then once Dyllis made it to the trees there were too many sharp sticks underfoot. Selkie's feet aren't used to sharp sticks.'

Myna's knees gave way beneath her, and she sank into the nearest chair.

'You and Dyllis took me from the shore. Even though I was there with my mother?'

Father cringed. 'She loved you, from that first moment. We both did.' He stopped, met her eye. 'We both do,' he amended. 'You know that, don't you?'

Myna's eyes stung as she shook her head.

'You may have thought you loved me, but you hated not being part of the town, living on the outskirts. And what about me? I grew up with no friends—always the outcast, always the focus of stares and whispers.' She wiped the tears building in the corners of her eyes. 'My own mother would have loved me. And I would have grown up as one of a group, not always the odd one out.'

'Myna—'

'If you and Mother had loved *me*, you would have sought out what was best for *me*. You would never have forced me into a life of your choosing. You would never have taken me from my family to begin with.'

She stood, and strode the few steps across the room to the door, slamming it on her way through.

      She was a selkie, was she? Selkies hadn't been seen since before she was born. Long extinct, her parents had told her when she'd asked about the tales. Ronan was from a larger town, further down the coast. He considered them folklore. How could she tell him they were real?

      How could she tell him she was one?

Chapter 12

Myna surveyed the room that had been her parents' bedroom. The kitchen furniture and items had been easy to sort through, the best items stored for when Ebba grew up, those still functional passed on to a young, soon-to-marry couple, the rest piled up on a bonfire heap.

But this room…Myna sighed. She should have dealt with it earlier, when they'd first moved Father out to live with them.

Now the room stank of must and mould, cobwebs gathered in all the corners and dust coated every surface and danced in the rays of light sneaking through the door.

Myna hadn't been bothered at the time. She

hadn't wanted to leave her active toddler and senile father in the care of any of the village women who claimed a friendship Myna still couldn't reciprocate. And she'd had such a strong aversion to the trudge back up the hillside, to the place she'd finally escaped from, that no amount of mental urging had broken through.

But now the man she'd called Father had died, and she could no longer put off this unpleasant task.

She turned to the chest of drawers as Ronan heaved the straw-filled mattress off the bed, disturbing a family of mice as he hauled it outside.

Myna opened the drawers, pulling out clothes, mouldy and motheaten. There was nothing salvageable here.

'We can't get the bed down the hill.'

Myna looked around to Ronan standing with a hand on the bed head.

'It's too heavy.'

Myna sighed and nodded. 'The rug seems to have survived," she said.

'We should take it out and clean it. Give it to someone who needs it. Better not leave it here to rot.'

Together, Myna and Ronan pushed the bed to one side to move it off the rug. There was a deep indent, where the floorboards beneath seemed to have caved in.

Ronan bent over to roll up the rug, revealing a broken floorboard beneath.

A waft of fresh sea air met Myna's nose, and there was a prickle on her skin as the hairs on the back of her neck stood on end.

'Looks like a hidey hole.' Ronan had dropped the rug, and stood by Myna, looking down at the broken floorboard.

'I'm sure it's not.' Myna backed away, picking up the end of the rug Ronan had dropped. 'It's just a loose floorboard.'

'There's no such thing as *just* a loose floorboard.' He grinned, bending down to examine it. He managed to wedge a finger into the crack and raised one end of the board ever so slightly.

'It's stuck. Can you grab me something to lever it with?'

Myna shook her head. 'There's nothing down there.' Inside her chest her heart was pounding so loudly, she felt sure Ronan must hear it.

'It won't hurt to check, will it? Maybe it's the

thing your father was always going on about. That your mother hid.'

Myna stopped in her tracks, fear almost knocking the breath out of her. He'd heard those conversations?

Of course he'd heard those conversations. How could he have missed them?

'Come on, Myna. Maybe it's the thing they stole from the sea. It could be worth a fortune.'

But Myna shook her head. 'Father was a demented old man. He didn't know what he was saying half the time. Let's just get this stuff out of here and go home.'

But Ronan wouldn't be turned away from his prize. He went outside himself and grabbed a narrow branch, taking it back inside to lever up the board.

Myna didn't want to see, and yet something compelled her to watch as Ronan pulled up the first board, and then began to work on another when it became evident whatever was underneath was too big to fit out through the gap.

'This board doesn't seem loose.' Ronan frowned, prying at it with the branch. He spun the branch around and wedged the thicker end underneath the floorboards.

'Perhaps I should come back with my tools.' His words were muttered, but Myna felt a stab of fear at the thought.

'It doubt it's worth it,' she said. 'It must've been under there for years. It's probably mouldy and rotten by now, if it hasn't decayed altogether.'

'No.' He shook his head. 'Can't you smell that? It smells…fresh. Like the sea.'

He returned his focus to the branch, and after a bit of pressure the next floorboard along lifted from the joist.

Ronan grabbed hold of whatever it was beneath.

'It feels like skin.' He shook his head. 'It can't possibly be skin—it'd be dry and brittle after all this time.'

Myna squeezed her eyes shut, her stomach churning.

Ronan removed another floorboard, and then Myna heard the slithering of something sliding against the boards. She opened her eyes. Ronan was pulling something huge and dark from underneath the floor. There was something stuck to it, and as Myna crept forward to see she realised it was a torn flour bag. A one pound flour bag.

Ronan ripped it away, and Myna knew with sudden clarity that the skin was once small enough to fit into the bag. That it had grown, as she had.

Ronan dragged it out onto the lawn while Myna held back the shriek that wanted to warn him; 'be careful, don't hurt it!'

Outside, it was easier to see. The skin was thick and rubbery, and damp to the touch. It was grey with a mixture of lighter and darker coloured splotches, and fine hairs all over. And heavy. It took all of Ronan's strength to drag it out onto the grass.

'This looks like a seal skin,' Ronan said, spreading it out on the grass. 'But it's the biggest one I've ever seen.'

Myna refused to touch it.

'I wonder how long it's been there for.'

His hands smoothed out across the skin, and a tingle travelled Myna's spine. She could *feel* Ronan's touch on her back.

You have one too. Wayanna's words echoed. *The human will have hidden it somewhere. If you find it, you can come home.* She shook her head, and backed away, tripping backwards to sit on the bottom step.

'And where did they get it from? It's in perfect condition. We could get a good amount of money for this at the market.'

Myna slid backwards up three stairs till she was sitting on the landing. It had shivered, she was sure of it, at Ronan's mention of the market.

'We should leave it here.' Myna clenched her hands into fists, fighting the urge to reach out and take it from him. 'Whatever it is, it isn't natural.'

Ronan laughed, but he soon stopped when he saw Myna wasn't joking.

'It's probably cursed. It's the reason I was an outcast my whole life. How else has it survived this long? Why else would it be hidden under the floorboards? We should put it back, now, before it ruins our lives as well.'

Myna blinked and tears spilled over her cheeks. She wiped them away angrily with the back of her hand.

'You believe that?' Ronan had dropped the skin, and was moving towards her, his brow creased. 'You think that this is the reason your parents were outcasts? You think this is…what? Magic?' He gave a hollow laugh. 'You sound like some of those superstitious old villagers.'

Myna shook her head. How could she tell him she knew what it was? That *magic* wasn't the half of it.

'You're serious, aren't you?' Now he was beside her, his arm around her shoulders.

'How else do you explain its condition?'

He shrugged. 'Your father would've salted it, he's not that foolish—'

'And salt preserves things for decades, does it?'

'I don't know. I've never left anything that long.'

'Does it look like it's been salted?'

'Well, no. But maybe the salt has dissolved. Maybe we got here just in time.'

Myna could hear from his tone he didn't believe his own words. She shook her head. 'We need to put it back and nail up those boards so nothing can remove them.'

The skin called to her. Even now she could feel its longing to be picked up and wrapped around her shoulders; its desperation to return to the sea. She shook her head again.

'Please, Ronan. Please. Put it back.'

Ronan looked from her to the skin and back

again. He almost agreed with her, she could see the disappointment in his eyes at giving up what he thought was a fine prize. But then the feeling from the skin changed, and Myna realised its longing was now being directed at Ronan.

'No,' he said. 'No. I think you're wrong this time, Myna, love. We need to take this with us. I'll peg it out in the shed; you won't even know it's there. And as soon as it's dry I'll sell it at the market. It won't take long. Pegged out properly it will dry soon enough. We'll get a good amount for it at market, you'll see. We can use the money to finish Ebba's room.'

Chapter 13

Myna crept out of bed, stumbling in the darkness as she crossed the day's clothes discarded on the floor. She was too tired for this. It had been a week's work, emptying her parents' home and shed, adding to the bonfire the things too far gone to save, and saving the things too precious to burn. She should be sleeping, and instead she tossed and turned in the narrow bed, finding no comfort in Ronan's arms, no soothing from Ebba's steady breathing across the room.

Outside, the air was chill, a halo around the moon the sign of tomorrow's frost—and something else? The old women said a ring around the moon was sign of upheaval to come, but Myna couldn't imagine any upheaval greater than that which already twisted in her gut.

A few short metres found her at Ronan's shed. The door always creaked and for a moment Myna hesitated, would it wake him? What about Eb? But the tingling down her neck and across her shoulders pushed all concern of that aside, and she pulled the door in one swift movement.

She held the door open, listening. Her heart was beating so loudly she wasn't sure she would hear anything over it, but after minutes passed with no movement, she decided all was clear and stole inside, fumbling in the dark to find Ronan's lantern, and strike a match.

The skin gleamed. If anything it looked wetter than it had that afternoon, when Ronan had declared that after a week it was finally, *finally,* starting to dry out.

Must be the size of it. His words echoed in her mind. *Would never've thought a skin would take so long to cure.*

Now she was here, face to face with this thing, this object that confirmed all the strangeness that had happened to her. It was a relief, in a way. It proved she had not crossed over into madness, that the conversations with the girl on the beach were real, and the skin she had then been shown— the skin that looked like this one—was real, too.

Repulsion fought with desire and she reached out; let one finger slide across the surface. A warmth tingled along her finger, and she spread out her hand, laying it flat on the surface.

It wasn't slimy, as she'd expected. It was damp, and warm despite the cold, and Myna wondered for a moment exactly what would happen if she put it on—what would that sensation be like? Morphing from one creature into another, losing limbs and gaining flippers, growing whiskers either side of a newly elongated nose.

'Can't sleep?'

She jumped, whirled around to see Ronan, bleary eyed, rugged up in his coat.

'I... ah. I... no. No. I couldn't sleep.'

'You're as intrigued by this thing as I am, aren't you?' He stepped into the narrow confines of the shed, and put an arm around Myna's shoulders. 'You've been keeping your distance, but you're just as curious.'

Myna felt a knot in her throat and nodded. What else could she say? How else would she explain being out here, examining it like this?

'Can we look at it in the morning though? I need my sleep.' He yawned as though to prove his point, and Myna allowed him to propel her back through the yard and into the house.

Could she do it? Could she take the skin and slip it on? What would she do then? Slip into the sea and never return? That's how all the myths went—when a selkie got her skin she went back to the ocean and never came back. But Myna had no memory of life in the ocean; she'd never even entered it, save that one fateful day when she learned how much her mother feared the salt water. That reaction had been enough to keep her away for good. What did the ocean feel like? How would she survive in a place that required her to catch fish with her mouth, to eat them raw? She shuddered. She couldn't do it. It wasn't her place, not anymore. For better or worse, when Dyllis had stolen her from the shore she'd committed Myna to a life on solid ground, surrounded by air, in a body that had legs and arms and hands and feet.

'Cold?' Ronan mistook her shiver and pulled her closer, rubbing one arm with his hand. 'Let's get back to bed.'

She nodded again, grateful for the arms he wrapped around her as she snuggled in close, but still unable to sleep with all the *what if's* circling her mind.

And then there was the girl on the beach, the one who had a skin just like hers. What would she say if she knew Myna was thinking of rejecting it? How would she feel to learn that her mother had decided to stick with the child she knew, the child she'd already began to raise, and neglect the child she'd been told had died?

Chapter 14

'You found your skin?' Wayanna's joy hit Myna with force and she took a step back as she shook her head.

Wayanna frowned. 'I can smell it on you.'

Myna stopped her head from moving.

'I—'

'You didn't bring it?'

Myna felt the nerves bubble up in her chest and she laughed. There was no way she was going to touch it again. But she couldn't say that to Wayanna.

'I can't carry that! You haven't seen it, it's enormous. So thick and heavy.' She shook her head again. 'I'd never get it here all by myself.'

'What about Father? He could help—'

'He doesn't know.'

Wayanna's eyes widened and Myna felt the all too familiar pang of guilt.

'How could I tell him? How could I explain all this? He doesn't even believe in selkies—'

'But you can show him otherwise.'

Myna shook her head again. 'You have no idea what I've been through. Your father is the only person who's ever been on my side. I couldn't bear to lose him. And I don't even know what life is like for you. I have no recollection at all of life below the waves. How can you expect me to long for something I don't even remember?'

Wayanna's eyes narrowed. 'But you do, don't you? You long for the sea, to swim in the waves. What is it you're afraid of, Mother? Are you afraid you'll lose yourself and never come back? I've seen you gazing over the water, and yet you've never even dipped your toe in. Why? You won't turn into a seal with the touch of the sea—you need your skin for that. Or perhaps you're scared of finding yourself and realising how fulfilling life could be if you actually followed your true nature.'

Myna kept shaking her head, trying not to

hear Wayanna's words. 'I can't go into the sea. My mother—'

'Your mother is out there, under the waves. Missing every moment she could be with you.'

The anger of a sixteen-year-old was too much for Myna and she fled back up the beach, slipping in the soft sand and stumbling over loose rocks.

'As if a child could understand,' Myna muttered to herself. But of course she couldn't. Of course her life under the waves would seem preferable to one above. She'd never understand that life above the sea felt normal to Myna.

And yes, Myna *did* yearn to swim, and now Mother was dead there was no reason not to, and yet... It was honouring her mother's memory, staying away from the waves. Her mother had done so much for Myna, endured the loss of community, suffered from the whispers and gossip of the villagers, just as much as Myna had.

The woman you call Mother *stole you.* A voice spoke in her mind. *She was ostracised because she stole you. Any suffering was punishment for her own actions. And she wasn't the only one who suffered, what about your family; your mother, your father, mourning the loss of their child. What about your daughter? You lost her because she looked different, ill-formed. She has grown up without parents because the human you insist on calling 'Mother' stole you.*

Myna closed her eyes, fighting against Wayanna's accusations in her mind.

She pulled her shawl tighter around her shoulders and increased her speed. It would be midnight soon. And Myna needed her sleep.

Chapter 15

Myna and Ronan sat together on the rocks, repairing Alfred's nets. Ebba played in the sand, right on the edge of the rocks. At the water's edge, other village children splashed and chased each other, and Myna wondered why Ebba didn't explore the ocean as the other children did.

'Does Ebba get her reticence of the water from me?' she asked, glancing at Ronan.

Ronan looked up.

'It might have something to do with it,' he said.

Myna squashed down her guilt and set down the net. She strode across the sand to her daughter.

'You want to paddle in the sea?'

Ebba looked down to the water.

'You and me, let's paddle our feet.' Myna held her hand out and Ebba glanced up, first at Myna's outstretched hand, and then at her face.

'But you don't like the sea, Mama.'

'But that doesn't mean you shouldn't like it, Eb.' Myna gave an encouraging smile, and Ebba stood, brushing the sand from her trousers. Holding hands, the two walked to the sea edge. They waited in the damp sand for the receding waves to turn tail and wash back up.

Ebba squealed and leaped backwards as the chilly water met her feet, but Myna held her ground. Once again, the waves receded and returned. Now Ebba was giggling, twisting her feet this way and that to sink her feet in the sand.

'Is this fun?'

'Yes!' declared Ebba, kicking her feet to splash Myna.

'Shall we go deeper?'

Now Myna was here she felt the pull to be submerged in the sea. The ocean was safe. It wouldn't hurt them. Ebba should learn that.

Ebba nodded, trusting.

Myna led her daughter deeper. But knee-deep

for Myna was waist-deep for little Ebba, and Myna had to hold her daughter's hand tighter lest Ebba be knocked over.

Ebba squealed again, but the sound had lost its joyful shriek and instead held a hint of fear.

'Mama!'

'Shh...it's all right.' Myna picked up her shivering daughter.

'I want to go back.' Ebba clung to her mother's shoulders.

'Just a little farther.' Myna cooed, taking another step, and then another.

Soon the water was around her waist, and then her chest.

'No more, Mama!' Ebba shrieked as the water splashed her face, and she tried to climb up her mother's torso to get farther from it.

'Shh...' Myna soothed. 'We're safe. The sea won't hurt us.' She took another step, and another.

'Mama!' Right in her ear, the scream snapped Myna from her trance and she looked at Ebba, red-faced and wet with tears and sea spray.

'Oh. I'm sorry, Eb.' She turned back to the shore, realising just how far out they'd ventured. Now she saw Ronan, trousers rolled above his knees, already shin deep in the water. The few other families on the beach had stopped and were watching her.

Heat rose in her face. Ebba reached out for her father as they drew closer, and clung to him, sobbing into his shirt.

'What were you doing?' Ronan was furious. 'Are you mad? Do you want her to be afraid of the sea as you are?'

Myna lowered her eyes. How could she explain she wasn't thinking about land at all, but about water and sea and life under the waves? How could she ever explain such a thing to him, without first explaining who she was, and what that meant?

He strode ahead of her across the sand, scooping up the net and basket. Myna retrieved their boots and followed behind.

Maybe I am mad. Tears welled. *Maybe Wayanna is a figment of my imagination.* She wished she could convince herself it was the case, that the appearance of the skin was just a coincidence, something her mind was using as evidence of a crazy story concocted by a mind desperate for answers.

Chapter 16

'Our daughter didn't die.'

They were the first words Myna had spoken in the two days since she'd tried to introduce Ebba to the sea.

Ronan's arm tensed. He lowered the teacup and dishcloth to the sink, but didn't turn around.

'She was terrified, Myna. You've probably ensured she'll never go near the sea again.' Now he turned, his jaw squared. 'But that's what you wanted, wasn't it? You hate the ocean, you always have. And you wanted to make sure she did as well.'

Myna frowned. 'What? No.' She shook her head. 'Not Ebba. Well, yes, Ebba. But the first one.'

A lump caught in her throat and she coughed to clear it. 'The one you and Oulde didn't let me see. The one you gave to the ocean.'

Ronan's face paled. 'What are you talking about?'

'I'm talking about our firstborn. I know she lived. Wayanna is the name she goes by now.'

'Wayanna.' Ronan shook his head. 'There's no one in the village by that name.'

'She doesn't live in the village.'

'Then where does she live? You barely leave the house, so how could you have met someone from farther away? How do you even know it's her, and not someone playing a cruel prank?' Ronan's voice rose as he questioned her, and she could hear the anger in it, and her anger rose to match it.

'How would anyone know our baby was a daughter? You got rid of her so fast you weren't even certain yourself!'

Ronan's mouth opened, then closed again.

'But how?' His gaze met hers, and Myna felt a pang of sorrow for the pain she saw. 'Oulde told me she wouldn't live, even if we kept her. She was so disfigured.'

'Disfigured?'

He looked up sharply. 'I told you. Her face was all...squashed.' He paused. 'You're telling me the girl who claimed to be her is properly formed?' His hands clenched. 'You've been tricked, Myna.'

Myna frowned, confused. But then everything made sense. 'She was born in her skin.'

'Her skin?'

'She's a selkie.'

'A selkie?'

'You know the stories.'

Ronan shook his head. 'And how is it that we have a daughter who's a selkie? Unless you had an affair with a seal-prince.' He laughed. There was no malice in it, no accusation. He didn't believe it at all.

'No.' She took the step across the room and reached out to grab her husband's hand, to make sure he was looking at her when she spoke, that he saw the truth in her face. 'I'm a selkie.'

His peered at her.

'That seal skin out there, the one that's the biggest you've ever seen, that hasn't dried despite being pegged out for over a month, that's my skin. I never knew I was selkie. Not till I met Wayanna, anyway. Dyllis stole me as a baby. I have no recollection of life under the sea, only of life on land, as a human.'

Ronan pulled out a chair to sit down, still gripping Myna's hand. 'You're telling me those stories are true?'

Myna nodded.

'You're saying you could wrap that skin around you and...what? You'd turn into a seal?' He scoffed at the thought, but even as he did his face grew serious. 'The stories tell that whenever a seal woman finds her skin she returns to the ocean. They say she's never seen again.'

'I don't intend to go to the ocean.'

'But you did, just the other day. Once you were in the water you didn't want to come back. Not even Ebba screaming in your arms was enough to get you to turn around.'

Myna took Ronan's other hand in her own, gripping his hands with hers. 'You know I've always felt a...a pull, to the ocean.' She looked down at their entwined hands. 'But I'm also terrified of it. When I'm in the water I can't stop. It's why I avoid it. I thought maybe I could show Ebba how much fun the waves were, but it was too strong for me.' She looked back up, meeting Ronan's gaze again. 'But if I stay out of the water, I can stay in control.'

She pulled away one hand to lay it on his cheek. 'I never want to lose you, Ronan. You have been my anchor these past fifteen years, and now I have Ebba as well. The two of you are the best thing that's ever happened to me. I won't give that up.'

'Not even to go home?' Ronan's voice broke and he turned his face away, blinking.

Myna gently turned his face back to her. 'This is my home. Here, with you and Ebba. This is all I know. I'm not going to risk that to venture out there. Not ever.'

Chapter 17

For days afterwards, Ronan's words echoed through Myna's thoughts.

Not even Ebba screaming in your arms was enough to make you to turn around.

He was right. She'd been so enamoured by the sea, so desperate to be immersed in the water, she hadn't been aware of Ebba's distress.

Her thoughts circled back to the only other memory she had of swimming in the ocean. It had been the same back then, hadn't it? And she didn't even have her skin with her. What if she'd given in to that impulse to dive down deep? Would she have drowned? Or would her seal family know, and come to help her?

I have to stay away from the water.

Myna stood outside Ronan's shed. She sighed, lifted the latch and stepped inside.

The skin was still stretched out, nailed to a rough wooden frame with a hundred tiny nails. She ran her fingers along the skin, fought the urge to tear it free and wrap it around her shoulders.

She took a deep breath, just as a shadow blocked the light. Ronan stood in the doorway, little Ebba in his arms.

'What are you doing?' His voice cracked.

'I need you to hide this.'

'Sorry?'

'I need you to roll it up and store it somewhere I will never find it.' It took Myna a moment to realise the wet on her face was her own tears.

Ronan reached out his spare arm and Myna fell into it.

'Are you sure?' His voice was subdued.

Myna ignored the growing heaviness in her heart and nodded. 'I'm certain.'

Part 3

Chapter 18

Years passed. Myna avoided the sea, staying well away from the shore, and if ever she wondered what Ronan had done with her skin, she pushed the thought away.

If she focused on what she had, she was happy.

And Ebba was happy enough, too. She went to school, made friends, told jokes and avoided chores. So far as Myna could see, Ebba carried none of the weight Myna herself had felt growing up.

She'd given her daughter a normal childhood, with two parents who loved her, and none of the secrets or shame hanging about, waiting to be exposed.

And she intended to keep it that way. The past could not be changed, but it could be forgotten. There was no reason for it to interfere in the life they had now.

ഽ

Myna wasn't sure how it happened.

The wind carried the singing from the beach, and it had been so long since she'd heard Wayanna's song, she was out of the house and down the path before she was fully awake.

It seemed foolish to turn around then, so she followed the path to the shore. The exertion warmed her, and she peeled off her jumper at the grassy edge, abandoning it on the sand.

Wayanna was already a seal, splashing back through the waves, but Myna called out anyway, distantly aware of the desperation in her voice, the loss she'd felt at not seeing her oldest child for such a long time.

She splashed into the sea.

'Wayanna!'

There was no response.

What more do I deserve? Abandoning her, out of my own fears, my own lack of control. The weight in Myna's chest pulled her down, and she sank to her knees, icy water swirling up and around her waist.

All the sorrow she'd bottled up welled up inside her: the guilt over abandoning this daughter as she attempted to raise the other; the strain of avoiding the ocean; the constant presence in her mind of her skin, hidden in regions unknown.

Her sobs were loud, but Myna didn't care. Who would hear her, all the way out here, at this time of night?

A smooth, wet shape slid past her in the water, and Myna gasped.

'Wayanna.'

A wet whiskered nose popped out of the water and Myna wrapped her arms around the seal's thick neck.

'I'm so sorry I didn't come back.'

The seal gave a couple of short, sharp barks and nuzzled closer.

Myna crooned a lullaby, something she hadn't sung in years. The seal was quiet and still in her arms.

When she stopped, Wayanna stretched out of the water to touch her—whiskery nose to damp cheek—and then slipped back into the water.

With a start, Myna realised how cold she was, how her clothes had soaked up the sea.

She stood and turned, but there was a shadow on the sand ahead, and for a moment she thought it was Wayanna, thought she'd swum in behind Myna and shed her skin, but then she saw the shorter nose of Ebba's face, and the hair pulled back in a ponytail as Wayanna's never was.

Her younger daughter's eyes were wide, and Myna felt a flash of fear. How long had she been standing there? What had she seen?

Myna surged forward and grabbed Ebba's arm. It was icy cold.

Ebba said nothing as Myna pulled her out of the surf, hauling her up when she tripped in the sand.

They reached Myna's jumper and Myna pulled it over Ebba's head. Myna pulled her daughter across the grass and along the rocky path, not stopping till she reached home.

Inside she called out to Ronan as she sat

Ebba in a chair and stoked up the fire. He brought blankets, and Eb gazed up at him in confusion.

'I'm all right,' she said, through blue lips. 'It's Mother you need to worry about.'

'Your mother is fine, Eb.'

'No. She fell into the sea. She was crying.'

'It's late, Eb. Let's get you warm, and into bed. We can discuss it in the morning.'

Myna pulled the bedroom door behind her, removing her wet clothes to pull on dry ones and climb under the blankets. Morning was far too soon as far as she was concerned. How was she going to explain this?

Chapter 19

The wash-house door creaked and Myna turned to see Ebba peering in.

'Have you finished your chores?'

Ebba nodded. 'I've cleaned the house and returned Alfred's nets. And Father had me deliver some fruit to Colleen.'

Myna nodded. 'Thank you. There's nothing more I need right now. You can have some time to yourself.'

Ebba nodded, but stayed in the doorway.

'What is it?'

'I want to talk about last night.'

'There's nothing to talk about.' Myna turned

back to her task, pulling a shirt out of the tub to scrub it against the washboard. 'It was a dream.'

'I mentioned it to Colleen.'

'What would Colleen know?'

'She said you had another child. A baby that died. She said the midwife took it. She said you used to go down to the shore, and gaze out to sea. She thinks the midwife must've given the baby a sea burial.'

Myna froze, her heart pounding, as Ebba continued.

'She said maybe you were still grieving.'

Myna forced herself to return to her task as Ebba moved closed behind her to put a hand on her shoulder.

'I...' What to say? *Yes, there'd been a child, and she'd been declared dead but actually was very much alive and lived with the seals?*

'I don't know what she's talking about.' Myna cringed at her thoughtless words.

'What?'

'I...I mean...'

'You know Colleen isn't the only one who's talked of such things. I've heard the stories.'

'What stories?'

'A child whose sudden appearance scared away all the fish, and then when a woman grown the sudden loss of her own child saw them return.'

'Where did you hear this?'

'It's a bedtime story a friend was told as a child. It was presented all rather mysteriously, I might add. I'd never have suspected it was connected to us, except her mother was horrified it was being told in front of me, and later, my friend explained why.'

'Oh, Eb.' Myna moved to put an arm around her daughter, but Ebba pushed her away.

'Don't comfort me about their *lies* while hiding your own. Don't make me believe I'm going mad. I was awake when I followed you to the beach. I know what I saw.'

Myna stared at her daughter, mute.

'You're not going to say anything, are you? You'd rather try and convince me I was sleep-walking or something, as if I often leave my bed in the dead of the night.'

Ebba slammed the door as she stormed off, and Myna's face flushed.

How had this happened? How was it possible she'd put one daughter offside just as she'd reconnected with the other? And how could she tell the truth without losing Ebba completely?

She leaned against the wall and slid down it till she was sitting on the floor. Myna wasn't exactly sure at what point they'd decided to keep this secret from Ebba, or why they'd thought it was a good idea at the time, but something in her felt compelled to keep it that way.

How is hiding a child's heritage beneficial to her?

Myna sank her face in her hands. She'd not known the truth of her own past for so long, and she'd almost lost her oldest child completely because of it. But the knowledge was of no use to Ebba, born without a skin. Ebba could never take seal form, even if she wanted to. Surely telling her she was descended from selkies was pointless?

But she had to tell Ebba the truth about the previous night. To continue to pretend otherwise was just going to hurt her daughter more. So how could she admit what happened, without alerting Ebba to the truth?

∞

101

'You're a selkie?' Ebba's mouth dropped open.

Myna's eyes widened. This was not how this conversation was supposed to go, though really, what other assumption was Ebba meant to make when she learned her sister was a seal. Myna raised her hands. 'I don't— that's not—'

Ebba raised an eyebrow. 'My sister is a selkie. You're a selkie.' She paused. 'So... does that mean Grandma was a selkie too? Did Grandpa steal her skin and hide it? Maybe we can find it, and use it?'

Myna choked on a laugh. 'Grandma wasn't a selkie, Eb.'

'Grandpa?'

'No.' Myna closed her eyes and took a deep breath. 'I never thought I'd have to share this story with you. I just sort of, locked it away.'

Ebba reached out a hand to touch her mother's shoulder. 'You can tell me. I'm old enough to hear anything you've got to say.'

Myna wished she shared the same cocky confidence as her sixteen-year-old daughter. She opened her eyes and met her daughter's gaze. 'I was stolen.'

Ebba's eyes widened and Myna's heart constricted. She closed her eyes, and when she

opened them, she focused her gaze on her cup of
tea.

'I've never…I've never said those words aloud
before.'

'Who…how…?'

'Dyllis, your grandmother… she couldn't have
any children of her own. One day she saw a selkie
on the beach, with her newborn baby. She took the
baby. The selkie wasn't used to running so she
couldn't catch up. You've heard the stories of how
the fish disappeared from the bay for all those
years. How the village almost died except for the
few who chose to stay on. The selkies scared all
the fish away, because of me. Because Dyllis stole
me.'

'Do you know this for sure?'

Myna shrugged. 'I know I was blamed for it.'

'And the fish came back when my sister was
taken back to the waves?'

'I don't know. Maybe. Maybe enough time had
passed. Maybe they gave up.'

'The selkies?'

Myna sighed. 'I don't know. I don't know any
of it. But the old folks always used to say that the
Sea bestows blessings and curses as She will. I

can only assume that when Dyllis took me from one of Her creatures that the Sea chose to curse. I don't know why the Sea has now returned her blessings, and I don't think it wise to question it.'

Ebba rolled her eyes. 'So, my sister. She was raised by the seals then? Does she know your parents? Have you met your parents?'

'No.' Myna shook her head, a weight growing in her chest. 'I never thought to ask about them.'

'How could you not have thought about that? You have to ask about them. She'll have to know.'

Myna nodded, a sinking feeling in her chest. Why couldn't people just leave the past to rest? What was the benefit of delving into it?

None Myna could see. The past held nothing but hurt, and pain, and she couldn't see how bringing it to the surface would help anyone.

Chapter 20

Myna pulled her shawl tighter around her shoulders. The path underfoot was familiar now, even in the dark, but with the questions whirling around inside Myna's head she found herself stumbling on every loose rock and pebble.

Have you met your parents?

Ebba's question replayed in Myna's head. Why had it not occurred to her to ask Wayanna about them? She supposed in the beginning the shock of learning her first daughter not only lived but was a selkie had been a bit much to take in, but why hadn't she thought of it afterwards?

You were too afraid to ask.

Myna felt a shudder travel her spine, but it

was too late to ponder that any further, for she was on the beach and Wayanna had seen her.

'You came again.' The smile spread across Wayanna's face.

'I have to ask you something.' Myna cringed as Wayanna's smile washed away, but Myna knew if she didn't ask straight away she'd lose her nerve.

'What is it?'

'My parents.' Myna took a deep breath. 'Do you know them?'

'I know your mother. Her name is Oulde. I don't know your father.'

'Oulde? My midwife?'

'Midwife? What's a midwife?'

'Someone who helps a woman in labour.'

Wayanna frowned. 'I guess so. She said she was there when I was born, so—'

Myna sank back into the sand.

'My mother was at your birth, and didn't tell me.'

Wayanna kneeled beside her and put a hand on her shoulder.

'Maybe she thought it would be too much.'

'Too much? My real mother attended your birth, and not only did she not tell me who she was, she told your father you would die and she took you away. My own mother stole my firstborn. Did she want me to suffer as she did? Does she think it's my fault I was taken?'

Wayanna shook her head 'No. No. It's not like that at all.'

Myna narrowed her eyes. 'Then what is it like?'

Wayanna was speechless, and Myna stood up, and turned to trudge back up the sand.

'No. Wait. Please.' Wayanna called after her. 'Your father. I didn't tell you what I know about your father.'

Myna turned.

'You said you don't know my father.'

'I don't, I…' She swallowed. 'Your father is human. Oulde still visits him.'

'Human?' Myna blinked. 'From around here?'

'I don't know.'

'He must be, if Oulde still visits him.' Myna closed her eyes, pain piercing her chest. 'He's never made himself known, either. Maybe neither of them wanted me. Maybe Dyllis ws right to take me.'

Wayanna wrung her hands. 'You don't know that. Oulde cares—'

'If she cared she wouldn't have stolen my first child. She would have come to tell me the truth herself. My father would have come to tell me the truth.'

'Maybe your father doesn't know you were taken.'

Myna snorted. 'In a village this size everyone knows everyone else. If a baby appeared out of the blue, he would know.'

'Maybe he didn't know he got Grandmother pregnant?'

'She still visits him. Why would she not have told him that?'

Wayanna shrugged. 'Maybe I misheard. Maybe he wasn't from here, maybe he died.'

'And do you have any excuses for my mother? She must see you leaving every night, yet she does not come with you.'

Wayanna looked down at her feet. She wriggled her toes, burying them in the sand.

'She doesn't know I've met you.'

Myna frowned. 'What do you mean?'

'I'm not supposed to be here. After you were taken, the selkies all agreed to stay away from the villages. We don't come to the shore here, it's too dangerous.'

'Then how are you here?'

'I'm fully grown now. I take my own risks.' Wayanna glanced up at her mother, defiance clear in her eyes.

'You sneak out? I thought seals all slept in a big huddle.'

'We're a big group, I could be anywhere in it.'

Myna shook her head. 'That still doesn't explain—'

'Oulde told me not to come. She said that telling you would only ruin your life; that you thought you were human and the humans hardly know about the selkies anymore, so I should just let it be. She said if you thought I was dead then my coming back would be too much for you.' It all came out as a rush, but now Wayanna stopped and looked at her mother. 'Was it too much? Should I have stayed away?'

Myna hesitated.

How much simpler her life would have been if she'd never known any of this! She realised she was already shaking her head.

'You needed to come. *I* needed you to come.' She paused. 'You have probably never experienced the longing for a lost skin, but all my life I've felt that something was missing. Because I met you, when I found my skin I knew what it was—'

'And yet you still didn't come back.'

Myna shrugged. 'I had a three-year-old daughter. I couldn't leave her behind. And what about your father?'

'So, you chose them over me?'

Myna winced. 'If I'd known you had lived I would never have parted from you. I would have chosen *you*. But I didn't know, they told me you were dead. I'd already missed your childhood, and you've grown up with no idea of your mother. I didn't want that for Ebba.'

'But *you* don't have any idea of you, and you won't until you come home and see what it's like to live in your own skin, free of all this human nonsense.'

'If you're right about my father then this 'human nonsense' is just as much a part of me as my skin. And if I have a daughter who cannot go below the waves, why should I part from her? You have a human father, and a human grandfather if what you say is true. Perhaps you should shed your skin for a while and join us here. Maybe you'll find you like it on land more than you think.'

Wayanna narrowed her eyes. 'I've seen and heard enough about landfolk to know I don't want to be one.'

'Perhaps the thought of being one of the seal-folk is just as repulsive to me.'

Wayanna's eyes widened and she gasped. Myna saw the welling in Wayanna's eyes in the moment before she turned and fled back down the beach, scooping up her skin where it lay and flinging it around her shoulders.

'Wait,' Myna called, chasing down the beach after her daughter. 'I'm sorry. Wait.'

But Wayanna was already in the water. She dived under the waves, and though Myna waited, Wayanna didn't resurface.

'I'm sorry,' she whispered, hoping the breeze would carry her message beyond the breakers.

With slumped shoulders, Myna headed for home.

She had no answer for Ebba, not really. A selkie mother, they already knew that. A human father. And a selkie daughter who wouldn't share her clandestine meetings for fear of...what exactly? Myna realised now she'd never really discovered the answer to that. Either way, she was no closer to meeting her mother, nor to learning her father's identity.

Ebba would just have to be happy with that.

&

Myna and Ronan sat on the veranda; Ronan sipping his cup of tea, Myna repairing one of Alfred's nets.

Ebba emerged from the hut carrying two cups of tea, one for herself, and the other for Myna.

They sat in silence a while, listening to the crickets, watching the sun drop lower in the sky.

Myna cleared her throat. 'I spoke with Wayanna last night.'

Ronan glanced up.

'Did you ask about your parents?' Ebba's excitement shone through.

'I did.' Myna took a deep breath, and looked at Ronan. 'She said that Oulde is my mother.'

'Oulde?' Ronan frowned. 'How do I know that name?'

'Our midwife. The woman who helped birth Wayanna. The woman who told you our baby was going to die and took her away.' Myna couldn't keep the bitterness out of her tone.

Ronan's frown deepened. 'She was your mother?'

Myna nodded.

'How did she know to come when you were in labour?' Ebba asked.

Myna looked at Ronan, who held her gaze, though he replied to Ebba.

'We'd thought we could manage the birth ourselves. But your mother's contractions were so strong, even from the start. And she didn't want Dyllis there, not if we could help it. So, I went to the pub and asked for a midwife. And Alfred told me to go home and wait, and not too long afterward Oulde arrived at the door.'

'Alfred?' Myna and Ebba questioned in unison.

Ronan nodded.

'How did Alfred know to find Oulde?' Ebba asked.

'Alfred's a fisherman,' Myna said. 'He would know them.'

'Let's go and talk to him.' Ebba stood.

Myna shook her head. 'We can't. Nobody

knows Wayanna comes to visit. We'll get her in trouble.'

Ebba narrowed her eyes. 'So, you're just going to give up?'

'It's not giving up, Ebba. It's…it's being patient.' Myna returned her attention to the net in her hands.

'Patient? For what?'

'One day Wayanna will be able to tell her family that she comes to see me, and they might come then.'

'You're going to wait for a maybe?'

'Yes.'

Ronan looked at Ebba. 'And you are going to wait until your mother is ready.'

Chapter 21

Ebba watched the receding back of Alfred from her vantage point on the front veranda. As usual, he'd delivered his fish; a great big cod this time, the biggest Ebba had ever seen. Myna could've made it feed the three of them for a week, and yet he'd still be back tomorrow with another one.

'What's he so interested in, anyway?' The words were muttered. Ebba would never speak them loudly enough for her mother to hear—she'd questioned Alfred's motives once and received a sharp slap across the cheek.

'Alfred is the only person who spoke to your grandparents and me after the villagers ostracised us,' Myna had said. 'He and your grandfather were good friends.'

But when Ebba had questioned others, no one of her mother's age remembered a friendship between the two men; just that Alfred had always delivered a fish to her mother, right up until his leg gave out and he couldn't climb that hill anymore. Now that they lived closer to the village, Alfred was able to deliver the fish again, though it always seemed to Ebba that this pained him; that he did it out of necessity and not because he wanted to.

Perhaps he does it for Oulde.

Ebba's eyes widened. That would make sense. He was a fisherman, and she was a selkie. Perhaps that is why Alfred had been the only fisherman all those years, because the selkies helped him catch fish when no one else could.

'You are going to wait until your mother is ready.'

Her father's words echoed in her mind, but Ebba dismissed them. Circumstance had revealed the secrets they knew so far. Who knew how long before Wayanna was ready to share the truth with her family? Ronan's parents had died long before Ebba was born. If she waited for Wayanna, Myna's parents could be dead by then, too. Ebba wanted to

116

know now.

She followed Alfred along the path. The scrub along the shore was sparse, the ground rocky and uneven, and it wasn't till they were a good way along that Ebba called his name. She didn't want her mother hearing.

'Wondered if you were going to let me know you were there, or if you were just going to follow me around all day. Wouldn't have been very exciting, you know.'

Ebba ignored him.

'I want to talk about my mother.' The breeze picked up, whipping a thick strand of hair from Ebba's ponytail across her face.

'Aye. And what about her?'

'You fetched the midwife for her, when Ronan came for help. Oulde, her name was.'

'I did. What of it?'

'Oulde took my sister away.'

'Aye. The child was ill-formed.'

'So the story goes.'

'You don't believe it?'

Ebba shrugged. 'I've heard other versions.'

Alfred watched her for a moment. Ebba couldn't read his expression and she wondered what he could possibly be thinking.

'Where might ye've heard these *other versions*? Seems to me there's only three people that truly know what happened that night, and you live with two of them.'

Ebba nodded. 'That's true enough. But I wonder about Oulde.'

Alfred frowned. 'What about her?'

'She might be able to tell me more. Like, where she buried my sister, so I can visit the actual grave, and not Mother's memorial cairn.'

Alfred shrugged. 'She might. She might not.'

'But you knew her. You *fetched* her.'

'I did.'

'So perhaps you could fetch her again?'

'And how long has it been since your sister's birth? It must be close to thirty years. What makes you think I would still know Oulde, or where she might live?'

'You still fish.'

'And what does that have to do with anything?'

'You've always fished. You've always had luck with your catch.'

'Aye.'

'Well…' Ebba frowned. 'The Sea, She's blessed you.'

'So they say.'

'And you do not?'

Alfred shrugged. 'What are you getting at?'

Ebba pursed her lips. Hinting around the edges was not getting her any answers.

'I know Oulde is my grandmother. And I know she's a selkie. And if you fetched her that night, then you must know how to fetch her again.'

Alfred's mouth dropped open. 'And how on earth do you know all that?'

'It's true, isn't it? You're not denying it.'

Alfred closed his eyes and sighed.

'As I said, thirty years ago. What makes you think seals live that long?'

'She's not just a seal, though, is she? She's a selkie. As far as I can gather, magical creatures always live longer than humans.'

Alfred opened his mouth, then closed it.

Ebba seized her chance. 'I just want to ask some questions. That's all.'

Chapter 22

'Of course I was the midwife. Who else would help an outcast?' Oulde took a sip of her water, the long sleeves of her coat draping on the table. 'Everyone else in town was too scared to go near Myna and her family. And the town had shrunk so much by that stage that there was no local midwife anymore, anyway. When your father came to the pub asking for help, Alfred came and got me.' Oulde smiled at Alfred, who had moved his chair back to sit against the wall, Oulde's seal skin rolled up by his side. 'I just told your father I was from the next town along. What was he to know?' She smoothed down the robe Alfred saved for her visits.

Ebba was fascinated by this woman. Her

grandmother. She must have been in her seventies, but she barely looked fifty. Her dark hair was long and streaked white-grey, and deep smile lines engraved her face. She smelled like warm sand and a sea breeze.

Oulde took another sip of the water from the teacup in front of her and continued. 'When your sister was born, with all the markings of a selkie, I almost couldn't breathe. To have a selkie born of a human father and part-human mother is such a rarity, and our numbers are not great. Too many have been killed by poachers after our skins, and with so many women being abducted over the years we haven't had the births we once had. And to have a baby taken too, well, that was devastating, and not just for me, but for the colony as a whole.' Oulde was slowly spinning the cup on the table, her fingers inching around the outside of the rim.

'I had to take your sister back with me. I could see the disgust on your father's face when he looked at her. Even if we'd removed the skin and revealed the beautiful human baby within, he would always remember. And it was clear he had no idea of your mother's heritage, and neither did she. So, I cleaned up your mother, and I took your sister away, and that was the one and only contact I had with your mother since Dyllis took her from me.'

Oulde's voice broke, and Ebba glanced up to see tears in the selkie's eyes.

'Dyllis may have stolen Myna's childhood from me, but I still got to see the birth of a grandchild. Your mother didn't want Dyllis there for that.' She gave a chuckle, but there was no malice in it. 'Everything else I know of your mother, Alfred's told me.' She looked affectionately at Alfred again, and he gave a weak smile in return.

'When he said your mother was pregnant again, after all these years, I wanted to come back. But your mother was part of the village again, and another woman had trained up to be a midwife. And then you were born; a healthy, happy, human baby, and I knew you would mend your mother's broken heart. All was well in the world.'

She reached out a gnarled hand. 'But I am glad you've learned the truth of your past. Though I understand why your mother would not want to.'

'Mother doesn't necessarily—'

'There is much pain in your mother's past.' Oulde didn't let her finish. 'She probably doesn't want to re-visit it again.'

'She visits my sister every night.'

Oulde's eyes widened, and Alfred sat up with a start.

'That's how you know.'

Ebba felt a pang of guilt. 'I'm not supposed to say anything.'

'But you already have,' Oulde pointed out. 'May as well tell us the full story.'

'Mother goes to the shore every night. She usually goes after I've gone to bed, but one night she disturbed me, so I followed her. I've always thought she was terrified of the sea, but she waded straight in.'

Ebba paused. 'She was crying, and singing, and then something came out of the water. It was dark, I couldn't see properly, but it made distinct seal noises.'

Ebba made eye contact with Oulde. 'I harassed her for days afterward, and finally she told me the truth, as she knew it. I asked about her parents, if she'd met them, and she hadn't and so she asked Wayanna the next time they met, and Wayanna told her about you. And then Father said that Alfred had fetched you for them, and so I came to ask Alfred, and he fetched you again.'

'She knows nothing about her father?' Alfred asked in a gruff tone.

Ebba turned to Alfred. 'Just that he is still alive, that Oulde still visits him.'

Alfred swallowed nervously, and Ebba's eyes widened. 'You're the one Oulde visits?' Her gaze darted from Alfred to Oulde and back again.

'Aye.'

'So, you are…you are my grandfather?'

His face seemed to flush. 'I guess so, yes.'

'And that's why you've been delivering fish all this time. You're not just a lonely old man with no children of his own.'

'What?'

'I have a grandfather. A living grandfather.' Ebba felt the grin spread across her face. She looked at him.

'Can I tell Mother?'

Alfred shook her head, and Ebba's smile fell away.

Before she could speak, Alfred did. 'It's my responsibility,' he said, 'and well past time I owned up to it.'

Chapter 23

Alfred spent the morning on his boat, line in hand.

The sea was a soothing balm to his nerves, and always had been. Today he'd told the seals he was there to think—he didn't want them herding great schools of fish his way.

It had been so many years since his confrontation with Dyllis and Duncan. He'd long since decided he would *never* have that conversation with Myna. He'd always assumed that if Myna was to learn the truth, it would be from them, not him, but they'd passed into the next realm years earlier, and if they'd shared any of the truth with Myna, she'd never let on.

When Dyllis and Duncan had passed, Alfred

had thought things too late. And how old was Myna now? Fifty or above, too old to be shocking with this information.

Too old for him, too, he thought with a grumble. What would this do to his heart, opening wounds he'd thought long since scarred over? Though he had to admit, the scars had already started to stretch with Ebba's prodding.

In a way it was good. She'd always looked at him with such distrust. To have her open to him now she understood the truth was most definitely a blessing. But how to share that truth to Myna?

He felt a nibble on the end of his line and by habit gave a short sharp tug. The line pulled taut and with a seasoned movement Alfred pulled it back in, wrapping it round the reel as he pulled in something weighty. He was more than happy to see a good-sized cod on the end and dropped it into the bucket before baiting the hook and sending it back out again. If he was going to have this conversation, he'd feel better arriving with a couple of good-sized fish.

∞

'She's mine!' Dyllis hissed the words, holding the baby close. Already Alfred could see the rash on the baby's face, separated from her skin too soon, swaddled in human fabrics her little body wasn't ready for.

'She's not yours, Dyllis. She belongs with the selkies.' Alfred kept his voice low, for he didn't want to scare the child.

'And what do you care about it?' Dyllis moved so the table stood between her and him. Her eyes narrowed. 'The rumours are true, aren't they? You're friends with them.'

Alfred refused to acknowledge Dyllis's words, but kept steady eye contact with her. He had to get the child back to Oulde.

He knew Dyllis was desperate; the whole village knew her struggles. And when she'd turned up with this baby it was clear where it had come from, though few but the fisherman openly acknowledged the selkies' existence these days.

The fact that Dyllis had been desperate enough to kidnap one of their infants told him all he needed to know about her state of mind.

'Have a think, Dyl.' He kept his voice steady. 'Have a think about what you're doing. How would *you feel if this were your baby—'*

'This is my baby!'

Alfred continued. '—and someone stole her from you?'

Dyllis clutched the baby closer.

'They're animals, Alfred. You know that. They just take our form sometimes. And we all know animals don't feel for their children the same way people do.'

'They're more than animals, Dyllis. They ain't no different from us.'

A movement at the door caused them both to turn. Duncan stood with the door open, sighed, and closed it behind him.

'Alfred,' he said with a nod.

'Duncan.'

'You're here about the baby.'

'I am.'

'The fellas on the boat say you've been having relations with one of her kind.' He nodded at the baby as he spoke.

Alfred winced at Duncan's choice of words.

Dyllis's head whipped back to look at him. 'That's why you're here, isn't it? It's her mother you're in bed with.' Her eyes widened. 'She's yours, isn't she.'

Alfred hesitated. Would any good come from sharing the truth? Duncan had been a good friend for many years. Perhaps it would help.

'She is.'

Dyllis's expression seemed to soften.

'Her name's Myna,' he added.

'Myna. I like that name. We might keep it.' Dyllis peered down at the child in her arms. 'She has your nose.' Her tone mocked. 'You should've taken the selkie's skin. That's how the tale goes, right? You take their skin, and they can't leave. If you'd done that you'd still have your child.'

'Give her back, Dyllis. Please.'

'If that selkie beast was a proper mother I'd never have been able to take the child in the first place. Maybe you should be looking to her for neglect rather than me for caring! You won't ever take this child from me now. She's mine.' Dyllis held the child closer.

'A baby ought to be with its mother. She's not even weaned!'

'I can take care of a babe just fine, Alfred, with or without its mother's milk,' Dyllis interrupted. 'And you can just wander off home now, and tell that *creature her baby's in safe hands.'*

Alfred opened his mouth to speak but Dyllis spoke again. 'And don't be thinkin' of comin' and taking her. I've hidden the skin so well, none of you are gonna find it, and if you take her, I'll destroy it.'

Alfred's mouth closed, and Dyllis laughed. 'They can't live without their skins, can they? Even when they're not wearing 'em, there's still a connection there. One can't live without the other.'

Duncan tilted his head towards the door, and Alfred followed Duncan into the yard.

'I had no idea the child were yours.' Duncan shook his head. 'I told her not to take it. I said it wasn't a good idea.' His eyes met Alfred's. 'She thought it were a gift from the sea. We've tried so hard, Alf. You've never seen the pain in a woman's eyes month after month, every time her bleeding comes—'

'No. But I've seen the pain in a woman's eyes when her baby is taken.'

A flash of guilt crossed Duncan's face. 'Yeah, well. You know I'd help you if I could. But I've no idea where the skin is, she hid it even from me.' He looked at Alfred again. 'She dotes on it, Alf. She'll raise it good. You know that. Best just accept what the tides have brought.' He shrugged. 'P'raps it's like Dyl said, you should've taken her skin. You slept with an animal, and didn't even bother makin' her human, marryin' her. A child ought to have two parents present, not one on the land and one in the sea.'

Duncan turned and went back inside. Alfred's shoulders sagged as he turned and began the slow walk home.

They didn't understand, either of them.

Oulde was no animal, and nor was she an object to possess. Alfred had refused to take her seal skin, even when she offered it. He knew he couldn't keep her from her beloved sea, no matter her love for him. Salt water flowed through her veins, as oxygen flowed through his.

He didn't know how to tell her he'd failed her, that he'd failed their child.

୫

Alfred set his cup of cold tea back in its saucer.

'So, you see, I'm your father. I tried to get you back, as best I could. And you know I never forgot you. I always brought the best of my catch, to make

131

sure you were fed properly, from the sea, like you ought to've been.'

He looked up from his tea.

Myna sat across from him, unmoving. Alfred didn't know what to do. Should he wait a while? Give her a chance to absorb everything he'd said, to ask questions? Should he leave? Should he have never come in the first place?

He was about to stand when Myna looked up. Her eyes were wet.

'Oh love, I've upset you. I shouldn't've come.'

'My mother? Do you…? Does she…?' Myna shook her head.

'Your mother loves you, Myna. She always has. She suffered so much after you were taken, and after all these years…' Alfred sighed. 'It's painful for all of us, but if you want to meet her—'

'I do.' Myna's eyes widened even as she spoke the words. 'I mean, if it won't be too strange, for her?'

Alfred shook his head, coughing to clear the lump in his throat.

'She'd love that.'

'You did the right thing, Alfred.' Myna reached out a small cold hand to cover his larger one. 'And

I thank you for it. You kept our family sane, growing up, when you were the only one to visit. It means so much to me, to know you've been watching out for me all these years.'

Chapter 24

'Does it feel better to know?' Ebba stood in the doorway after Alfred left, watching her mother wash the dishes.

Myna paused and turned to glance at Ebba before returning to her task.

'It does, knowing the truth now. But I wonder what's the point of it? Does it change anything?'

Ebba frowned. 'Of course it does. You know your parents, now. And they know Wayanna knows. It's all out in the open. There are no secrets.' She crossed the room and picked up the tea towel to help with the dishes. 'You still have some of Grandpa's old trunks, don't you? Have you gone through them yet? Perhaps your skin is in one. We could find it, you could—'

Myna was shaking her head. 'I can't, Ebba. I can't go back to the sea. I can't leave you or your father.'

'It wouldn't be leaving. It would just be for a visit. You could come back.'

'Don't you remember the old stories? The selkie women never come back.' Myna was almost pleading. 'Once a selkie is back in her skin she never returns.'

Ebba scoffed. 'That's story, Mother. Besides, in those stories the women were taken as adults, from their *home*. You have no recollection of the sea at all. And Oulde comes back. She's never left Alfred.'

'That's different, Eb. She's never had her skin taken from her, she comes of her own free will. And she doesn't stay, she visits.'

Myna watched her daughter as she absorbed her words.

'You think you'd abandon us?'

Myna took a deep breath. 'I know I would.' She turned to her daughter. 'There's a memory you seem to have forgotten, for which I'm ever so grateful.' She took Ebba's hand. 'When you were about three years old, I was worried you were afraid of the sea, and I wanted to teach you that the ocean was a safe place. But once I was in the water, I lost control.'

∓

Ebba sat on the stony shore, the cold seeping into her backside and putting an ache in her bones.

'Where could it be?' Her words were muttered, there was no one to hear them, but she often found if she asked aloud the answer presented itself.

She'd searched the remaining trunks of her grandfather's, but they held few items; Grandma's crockery, a single water-stained photograph of some old people Ebba didn't recognise, a fine woollen shawl, a couple of books, her mother's childhood doll, and Grandfather's thick oil-skin coat. There was certainly no skin there.

Nor had there been any sign of it in Grandfather's still empty cottage. Nothing but dust mites and rats inhabited that space now, and the shed was the same.

She didn't know where else to look. Would Duncan have hidden it further afield?

'Dyllis has hidden it even from me.' That's what Duncan had told Alfred. So Grandfather didn't hide it then, Grandma did. And what hope did Ebba have of finding something hidden over fifty years ago, by a grandmother who'd died before Ebba was born?

A shadow crossed Ebba where she sat and she started. She realised the sun was already disappearing in the west, the evening star shone brightly in the eastern sky.

'Sorry, I didn't mean to startle you.' The shadow spoke, and Ebba realised it was a woman. Then her eyes adjusted to the glare, and for a moment she couldn't speak. The figure before her shared her own long dark hair and grey eyes. It was like looking at her reflection in a pond.

'You're Ebba.'

Ebba nodded, still mute.

'I never knew we looked so much alike,' the woman said. 'I'm Wayanna. Your sister.' She frowned. 'Mother has told you about me, hasn't she?'

'Oh, yes.' Finally something dislodged in Ebba's throat. 'I know all about you.'

'Oh?' The brief flash of relief across

Wayanna's face turned into a frown, and Ebba cringed at her choice of words.

'Sorry. I didn't mean...It's just...Yes. She's mentioned you. I know about our history, what happened to you, and her.' Ebba trailed off. She'd not ever thought to actually meet her sister herself, and now she wondered why. Fear? Jealousy?

Ebba realised Wayanna was watching her and opened her mouth to speak again. But Wayanna got in first.

'Why have you come to see me? You are waiting for me, aren't you?'

'I...' Ebba paused. 'I'm not really. I was just sitting here. I didn't realise...the afternoon got away from me.' She gestured to the west, where the sun had now set.

'Oh.'

The disappointment was clear, and Ebba felt awful.

'I've been searching for Mother's skin,' she said. Anything to change the subject. 'I've searched through Grandfather's things, even his old cottage, his work shed, everywhere I can think of. But it's not in any of those places. And sitting here I realise Grandma hid it from everyone, even Grandpa. But she died before I was born, so I have no idea where to start looking.' Ebba realised she was babbling, and stopped.

Wayanna gave her a curious look. 'Mother already found her skin,' she said. 'She found it years ago, when you were young. But she put it away. She refused to wear it.'

'What?' Ebba felt her mouth drop open.

'You didn't know?'

Ebba shook her head.

'She said she couldn't leave you, or Father. She suggested I shed my skin and join you on land.'

The resentment was clear in Wayanna's voice, and Ebba wondered at the jealousy she'd felt earlier. What right did she have to be jealous of a sister taking their mother's time? Ebba had all day of her mother's time, all her life with her.

'I'm sorry,' Ebba said.

'Don't be.' Wayanna offered a small smile. 'You got something I couldn't have, and I got something you couldn't have.'

'What have you got that I haven't?'

'My own skin.'

Chapter 25

'You already have it.' Ebba found her mother donning her coat, ready to head out the door to visit Wayanna herself.

Myna blinked at her, her face blank.

'I spoke to Wayanna. She said you already have your skin.'

Myna shook her head.

'Don't lie to me!' Ebba's throat was raw from the fury.

'I'm not lying, Eb.' Myna closed her eyes and Ebba realised how tired her mother looked.

'But Wayanna said you'd found it.'

'I did.' Myna nodded. 'But I don't have it

anymore.'

Ebba frowned. 'Then where is it?'

'I asked your father to hide it.'

Ebba's mouth dropped open for the second time that night. She wasn't sure she understood the words escaping her mother's mouth.

Myna sighed, removing her coat and hanging it back up on the peg.

'Come and sit down,' she said, removing the hot kettle from the hob, and putting some tea leaves in the pot.

'I've already told you what happens when I go into the sea without a skin. Imagine what would have happened if I'd had one. I'd be gone. You would've been left, at three years of age, without a mother. Your father without a wife. I couldn't do that to you, or him, or to me.'

'What do you mean?'

Myna sighed again. 'I missed seeing one daughter grow up. I didn't even know she was alive until I had you. I know that if I go back to the sea I won't return; generations of stories can't be wrong about that. I couldn't miss those years with you.'

'And what now?' Ebba put her hands on her hips. 'I'm grown up now. There's nothing to stop you now.'

Myna shook her head and Ebba realised there were tears in the corner of her mother's eyes.

'What else will I miss? Seeing you marry, meeting your children? I discovered as an adult that my family was not mine—that I'd been stolen from my true family. How can I leave the family that *is* mine, the husband I love, the daughter—my own flesh and blood—I gave birth to?'

'You'd be going back to family.'

'Family I don't know.' Myna shook her head. 'Why are you pushing this? Do you want me to leave?'

Ebba shrugged. 'You're always so sad. All my life you've been sad, always yearning for something more than Father and I can give. I used to think if I changed you'd be happier. Can you imagine how good it was to learn that your sadness was nothing to do with my lack? And now there's a solution. Your yearning could come to an end.'

But Myna shook her head again. 'Don't you see? I would always be yearning, if not for the sea, then for you and your father. I don't want a split life —half in the sea, and half on land. I have to pick one. And *this* is the one I've chosen.'

'You've always lived a half-life, Mother. Your body may be on land, but your heart is always in the ocean.' Ebba crossed her arms. 'You're just afraid, and you're using Father and me as an excuse.'

She turned and stormed back out the door, winding her way along the track, away from the beach, tears pouring down her face. *Why can't she see? Why do I have to be mother to my own mother?* As Ebba threw herself to the ground, rolling onto her back to gaze up at the stars, she knew one thing. If she had her own skin she'd be joining her sister, not pining away on land making everyone else's life a misery.

Chapter 26

A shiver travelled Ebba's body as her father heaved the skin down from its hiding place.

It pulsed. She could feel it from where she stood, a good few feet away. She took a step forward, reached out a hand, hesitated, and glanced at her father, who shrugged his shoulders.

At first touch a spark zapped her fingertips, a tingle that travelled the length of her arm, and she shivered.

'Should've told you to bring a coat,' her father said apologetically.

'It's not that.' The cave *was* cold, but the shiver was most definitely from the skin. She couldn't take her eyes off it. It was thick and warm, despite being stored in a damp, wet cave. Her skin began to itch.

It was calling to her.

'Don't you start looking at it like that,' Ronan warned. He allowed Ebba to unroll it a little way. 'That's how your mother used to look at it, all longingly, as if it were half her heart. I'm sure she still pines over the damn thing.'

'Maybe so,' Ebba replied. 'But she chose you over it. Even now she's not interested in seeing it again. She doesn't want to know what you've done to it. It's as if she's scared of it or something.' Ebba examined the skin more closely, before Ronan rolled it up and heaved it up into the high rocky ledge, out of sight of anyone who might venture in.

'Right,' he said, more grunt than spoken word. 'Well then, let's go.'

'Have you ever thought about giving her the skin, to see what she would do with it?'

Ronan shook his head. 'I don't need to. I know what she'd do. She'd be gone, Eb, she'd leave us behind without a second thought.'

'Is this because of what happened when I was three?'

'She told you?'

Ebba nodded. 'That's her excuse, too.'

'And you're still asking about this? Do you want your mother to leave?'

'Of course not!' Ebba sighed. 'But she's always so unhappy, surely you see that.'

'Of course, I see it!'

'Don't you want her to be happy?'

'Of course I want her to be happy. But Eb, I honestly don't think she would be. She loves us both; she'd miss us terribly if she was out there.' He nodded in the direction of the sea.

'Then why not give her the skin? If she missed us so much, she'd come back.'

Ronan frowned. 'Do you want to test your mother?' He put a hand on Ebba's shoulder. 'It doesn't matter how much she loves you, Eb. Being out there is her natural state; you can't fight that, no matter how many people you miss.'

'So, you'll just hide the skin away from her forever?'

He shook his head. 'I love your mother, Eb. You know that. You can't imagine my relief when she asked me to hide that damned thing. Every day I wake up wondering if today will be the day she wants it back. Because all she has to do is ask, and

I'll retrieve it. It would break my heart, but if that's what she wanted...' His voice broke. 'But for now she wants me to keep it hidden, so that's exactly what I'll do.'

Chapter 27

Ebba stood on the beach, a light breeze tickling the loose hairs around her face. In the west a faint band of blue showed where the sun had been, and above her the first stars twinkled.

The wash of the waves on sand blocked out most sounds, but still Ebba heard the slap of feet against sand. She turned.

'Hello, Wayanna.'

Wayanna tilted her head to one side. 'You came back.'

Ebba nodded. 'I wanted to meet you. Properly, I mean. Last time...' She shrugged. 'Well, last time was a bit of a shock, and I think I offended you.' She glanced up to catch her elder sister's gaze. 'I didn't mean to, you know. I just didn't think. It never occurred to me to come before. I don't know.' Ebba looked out to sea, frustrated she couldn't say what she wanted to. She shook her head. 'But you're my sister, so we should make an effort to get to know one another, shouldn't we?'

Wayanna nodded. 'I've been hoping for that ever since I learned of your existence.'

'And how long has that been?' Ebba raised an eyebrow.

'Hmm...' Wayanna pursed her lips. 'I think you were three?'

'Three?' Ebba's eyes widened. 'But that's thirteen years ago!'

Wayanna nodded again. 'Mother didn't want to leave because of you. That's what she told me, she wanted one of her daughters to grow up knowing their mother.'

'Ha!' Ebba scoffed. 'She doesn't want to leave because she's afraid. She's still using that excuse: 'What about seeing my grandchildren?'' Ebba put on her mother's voice.

Wayanna cringed.

'Shame she doesn't worry about her other grandchildren.' It was muttered, but Ebba heard it.

'You have children?' she asked.

Wayanna nodded.

'Mother never told me that.'

'She doesn't know. She's never asked.'

'Oh.' Ebba peered at her sister. The moon had risen now, full and round above the horizon, bringing Wayanna's eyes starkly into contrast. Her hair glistened wet in the moonlight as she shrugged.

'It doesn't matter. It's different for seals.'

'Different? How?'

'We aren't family oriented, like humans. No. That's not right. We are. But the whole colony is one big family. And our children grow up fast.'

'How many children do you have?'

'I've birthed ten. The oldest have their own pups now.'

'Mother is a great-grandmother.'

Wayanna shrugged. 'In human terms, I guess. But Mother never asks about my life.' Wayanna's mouth was set in a line.

'What do you talk about?'

'You, Father. Whenever I start talking about my life she cuts me off, suddenly has to leave.'

Ebba took a step closer. 'I'm sorry to hear

that,' she said. 'I'd like to hear more about your life. What's it like living in a seal colony?'

A faint smile turned up the corners of Wayanna's mouth.

'It's chaotic,' she said. 'There's hundreds of us, sleeping on the islands just off the coast. We have a leader, of sorts. Caelan, his name is. There's a seal who follows him around, Maggie. Some say she used to be a human, and he rescued her from a miserable life, but I don't know. She's definitely not like the other seals though. They're both from further south, but when the colonies diminished we all joined together. Safety in numbers, you see. When all the bulls fought for leadership Caelan turned out to be the strongest. He's getting on a bit, but he's kept us safe all this time, so we still look to him, even though some of the younger bulls are stronger now. There's not much else to our life. We sleep up on the sandy beaches, all huddled in together for warmth. But during the day we're all out at sea, hunting and fishing. Or just playing really. Once you've had your fill for the day there's no other work to do.'

Ebba's eyes widened. 'No school or chores?'

Wayanna laughed. 'What seal needs school?

We teach our young how to catch fish when they're first weaned. They don't need to know anything else.'

'That would be nice,' Ebba mused, gazing out to sea. She glanced back at Wayanna. 'So, I'm an aunt? How old are your children?'

'Well. It's not quite the same out there, in the sea. Oulde explained to me how families work here, but my oldest children are already adult seals. If we don't change often, we take on more seal traits. Taking human form slows our development.'

'But your youngest then? Is it still a baby?'

Wayanna smiled. 'She is. Just a few months old.'

'Why don't you bring her with you?'

Wayanna's face clouded again. 'I can't. Humans haven't treated seal-folk well. It started before Mother was stolen, killing seals for their skin and oil. But the theft of a baby was the last straw for our colony. I've seen the sorrow Oulde suffers. I don't want to risk experiencing that myself. We don't come here now; we avoid anywhere inhabited by humans. '

'Except you and Oulde.'

'Yeah, well...' Wayanna shrugged. 'I had to

find Mother. Being taken myself seemed like such a small risk, and I figured it would help me find her anyway, if it happened.'

'Do you think it was worth it?' Ebba asked. 'Finding Mother, I mean.'

Wayanna looked up at the moon. 'It has been good knowing her over all these years. Interesting to learn of the lives of humans, and Mother's fears and joys.'

'She shares that with you?'

Wayanna laughed. 'Not exactly. Over the years I've learned to read her expressions. I can hear when she's defensive about something, I know when she's angry, though she tries to hide those emotions. But emotions belong to the watery realm, and I am a creature of that realm, so I can read them easily.' Wayanna glanced at her sister. 'Our mother is quite determined to keep her distance.'

Ebba gave a wry smile. 'Our mother is terrified of everything she doesn't know. If she gets close to you she'll have another reason to return to the sea, and she doesn't want to have any reasons to do that.' Ebba paused. 'If she knew about your children she'd have a very big reason to request her skin back and return to the ocean.'

'Request her skin back? What do you mean?'

Ebba sighed. 'She asked Father to hide it.'

Wayanna frowned. 'He took her skin? I thought he was different—'

'He didn't take it, she gave it to him. It was too much of a temptation, having it near, so she asked him to hide it for her.'

'She didn't want it?'

Ebba shrugged. 'Father showed it to me. It isn't even mine and I could feel how alive it is. If that's only half what Mother feels...' Ebba shivered. 'I can't imagine how she resists it at all.'

She looked up to see Wayanna looking at her strangely. 'What?'

'If you felt that, you can wear it.'

'What?' Ebba repeated.

'If you feel a connection to the skin, you can use it, too.' The light in Wayanna's eyes brightened. 'You could come with me. Meet the colony. See how we live.'

Ebba's breath caught in her throat. 'Mother's skin would work? For me?'

Wayanna shrugged, a smile stretching across her face. 'Only one way to find out.'

Chapter 28

Wayanna's words echoed in Ebba's mind for days afterwards.

Wear Mother's skin? She'd not ever thought about visiting her seal family. She wasn't born with a skin. She knew such an idea was impossible.

But now...Wayanna had planted a seed Ebba couldn't shake.

Wear the skin. Become a seal, just for a little while.

She hadn't been born to the waves, Ebba told herself, so she wouldn't be compelled to stay. Being on land was her natural state, and her father said you couldn't fight your natural state. She'd have no trouble coming back. And she wouldn't be stealing the skin, just borrowing it. That's all. Borrowing.

She'd meet her seal-family, experience their way of life, and return home. Maybe it would even encourage her mother to visit and meet her grandchildren.

Ebba nodded to herself, her thoughts certain. She would borrow the skin, visit for a while, and come back.

She closed her eyes and took a deep breath to quell the nerves flitting about in her stomach. She could smell the sea so strongly, despite being some distance away. And the waves crashing on the shore were all so clear. Had it always been so clear? She felt as though her senses were suddenly attuned to the ocean, she could imagine, now, the sun filtered through sea water, crystal clear to her seal eyes, not fuzzy as when she opened her human ones beneath the waves.

And the feel of the water on her skin, that would be different too, the weightlessness of moving through the ocean.

Ebba felt the call with every cell of her body. She had to experience it, just for a little while.

'Wayanna said to say hello.' Ebba picked another juicy red raspberry from the cane and dropped it into her basket.

'You saw her again?' Myna was on the opposite side of the row, barely visible through the leaves.

Ebba nodded, though she knew her mother couldn't see. 'I thought I should get to know her, seeing as she's my sister.'

She heard Myna's sigh though the canes. 'Yes. Well. It was hard to know what to do when you were younger. I didn't know how you'd react when you learned you weren't an only child, or that your sister lived most of her life as a seal.'

Ebba took a step along the row to reach the next lot of berries. A question burned her tongue, but she didn't want to ask until she could see her mother's face.

'Were you worried I'd tell other people? Just when things were getting back to normal, just when you were making friends. I probably would have; children don't seem to be able to keep a secret. Everybody would have known.' Ebba babbled to fill in the silence.

Myna sighed again. 'Probably, Ebba. Yes,

there's a good chance of that.'

They'd reached the end of the row now, and Ebba could see the furrows between her mother's eyes and across her forehead. Perhaps now was not the best time, but she couldn't seem to stop herself.

'Did you know Wayanna has children?'

Myna's eyes widened.

'She never told me that.'

'You never asked.'

'Well...' Myna looked down at her half full basket. 'I never thought she'd have anything of interest to share. What do seals do all day anyway; swim, eat fish? I never thought of family.'

'She's twenty-six, Mother. And she's part human, they all are. They're not *just* seals. And even if they were, seals have babies too.'

Myna turned to the next row, suddenly intent on filling her basket.

'Don't you want to know anything about them?' Ebba asked. 'They're your grandchildren, too.'

Myna's surprised glance told Ebba the thought had not occurred to her, but when Myna went back to picking Ebba realised her mother *didn't want* to think about it.

'I know I've been a disappointment to you, as a mother,' Myna began. 'But if you're telling me this because you want me to leave, I won't. There's your father to think of, too. His heart would be broken if I went.'

'That's not it at all.' Ebba frowned. She wanted to explain, but Myna had already turned and was walking along the path back to the house.

Ebba dropped to the ground, slamming her basket down as she did so.

She can be so infuriating! Why couldn't Myna see that all Ebba wanted was to have a proper family, with a mother who was present whenever they were together, and not permanently somewhere else?

She took a deep breath. The conversation had confirmed one thing. Myna would not be wanting her skin anytime soon. And if grandchildren couldn't tempt her, the thought of meeting extended family was enough to tempt Ebba.

I gave you the chance, Ma. She got up and strode back towards the house. *And if you aren't going to take it, I am.*

Chapter 29

Myna arrived home to a blazing fire and the delicious waft of stew. Ebba had set at the table, with a plate of freshly baked buns in the centre.

'What's this for?'

Ebba's face was flushed, yet the room didn't seem so hot to Myna.

'I just thought I'd cook us a meal before I go.'

'Go where?' Myna sat at the table, just as Ronan came through the door.

'What's this?' he asked.

'Ebba has decided to cook for us before she *goes*.' Myna emphasised the last word.

Ronan raised an eyebrow. 'Where are you going?'

'I'm off to spend some time with Wayanna.' Ebba dished up the stew and sat at the table with her parents.

Myna took a bite. 'This is delicious. We should get you to cook more often.' She looked approvingly at her daughter.

Ebba seemed to blush, but it was hard to tell with her already red face.

'I agree,' Ronan said.

Ebba tore a bun in half, slathering it with butter before dipping it into her stew. She seemed particularly intent on eating, and Myna felt a flush of discomfort. *Something's not right.* Myna took another mouthful of stew, glancing between her husband and her daughter. She knew her husband well enough to see he was completely oblivious to anything out of the ordinary, while Ebba avoided making eye contact and ate her tea so fast she was sure to get indigestion.

'Everything all right, Ebba?' Myna asked.

Ebba glanced up. 'Sure. Everything's good.' Her words were too clipped to be true, but Myna's question had succeeded in alerting Ronan that something was up.

'Anything you want to tell us?' he asked.

Ebba looked from one parent to the other. 'Wayanna's going to take me to the colony. I'm going to see how she lives.'

Myna raised an eyebrow. 'How, exactly, are you going to do that?'

Ebba took a deep breath. 'I'm going to use your skin.'

Myna dropped her spoon, and it clattered against the bowl and table.

Ebba reached out to grab her mother's hand. 'It's all right. I'm coming back, I promise. It's just going to be a short visit.'

'But—' Myna couldn't find the words.

'I don't think you can use your mother's skin, Ebba.' Ronan kept his voice calm, though his brows were furrowed. 'I've never heard of that in any of the stories.'

Ebba shrugged, though Myna could see Ronan's words had upset her. 'Wayanna thinks I can. It's worth a try, anyway. But I'm more human than not.' She glanced up, her gaze flicking between Myna and Ronan again. 'You don't need to worry if it does work. I'll be back.'

Ebba pushed her bowl away. 'I should get going. Wayanna will be waiting.'

Myna looked at Ronan.

'Wait,' Ronan began, but Ebba merely kissed him on the cheek and raced out the door.

'Do you think she's telling the truth?' Myna asked, her gaze meeting Ronan's.

'I don't know.' He shook his head. 'But surely if the skin is yours, you're the only one who can wear it?'

Chapter 30

Ebba struggled across the soft sand. The skin was heavier than it had been when she'd dragged it down to the house; it seemed to grow thicker and damper the closer they drew to the sea.

Her back ached and she shifted it, yet again, from one shoulder to the other. To start with she'd been careful not to let the skin drag across the rough scrub, worried about tears and scratches. As it grew heavier she'd stopped being so precious with it, and now she was on the sand she allowed a good part of it to trail behind her.

'I thought you'd be here before this,' Wayanna's voice called out of the darkness.

'This damn thing's heavier than I expected.'

As she spoke she felt a shudder move through the skin.

'I'd be careful if I were you,' Wayanna said. 'You're to live in that for the next while.'

'You speak as though it's a separate thing. Aren't skin and person connected?'

Wayanna shrugged. 'Separate parts of a whole, perhaps.'

Ebba began to unroll the skin. It was like a cloak, except the hood was a face and the bottom didn't flare out but instead tapered down to a narrow, hood-like hollow, just above the tail.

The skin was warm, and Ebba felt it quiver with excitement as it sensed how close it was to the sea. She'd felt that excited energy growing every step of the way, so much so that in her own stomach little schools of fish were darting about, making her feel seasick.

'I just wrap it around myself?' Now she was faced with the reality, Ebba wasn't so sure she'd made the right decision.

'Well, you ought to take off your clothes first.' Wayanna grinned. 'They won't be comfortable underneath the skin.'

The last thing Ebba wanted to do was get

undressed, but she nodded, took a deep breath, and pulled off her jumper.

'It's so cold!'

'You won't be, in a minute.' The light was back in her sister's eyes, and Wayanna moved in close to help Ebba with the skin.

'Just wrap it like this, and pull the mask over your head.' Wayanna pulled the skin tight around Ebba's shoulders, then the mask over Ebba's face. Everything went dark, and Ebba's skin tingled, and her chest constricted. The skin closed around her and she fell to the ground, her lungs fighting for air. The damp sand clung to her stomach and chest as she struggled, but then her face fused with the mask and she could breathe *and* see again, though everything was distorted, taller and larger than she was.

It took her a moment to realise the pale spindly things in front of her were her sister's legs, but by then they had gone and instead she was eye-to-eye with another seal.

Wayanna gave a joyful bark and lolloped towards the sea. Ebba understood the 'come on', and followed behind, clumsy and awkward in her new form.

The awkwardness lasted the distance to the water. As soon as Ebba was deep enough the water held her, and she understood for the first time the freedom of this weightlessness as she and Wayanna frolicked in the waves.

She dived down deep, her attention taken by a school of darting fish, and she followed them, opening her mouth to capture and swallow a small fish whole, savouring the soft texture and salty taste.

Joy swelled in her chest, and she leaped for the sky, breaking out of the waves and twisting to dive deep again.

She repeated the process, but this time a light caught her eye on the shore. She returned to the surface and floated there, watching and curious.

'Ebba!' The call echoed out across the waves. 'Eh-bah!'

Wayanna swum up next to her. Ebba could understand every word, even though Wayanna spoke in barks and snorts and whines.

'Did you tell them?'

'I tried. They didn't want to hear.'

'Do you want to go back?'

Ebba shook her head. 'Not yet.' She gave

Wayanna a friendly head-butt and dived back under the water.

'This way,' Wayanna barked, darting off to Ebba's right. 'Best follow me, sis. At least till you learn where you're going.'

Ebba grinned and twisted through the water, marvelling at the ease of movement. This felt wonderful.

Chapter 31

Myna stood on the beach, unable to comprehend what the evidence seemed to tell her.

Ebba had gone. She'd taken Myna's skin—she'd been able to use Myna's skin! And now she was out there, gambolling among the waves with Wayanna.

After Ebba had left, Ronan had led Myna to the cave, showing her the now empty ledge where he'd hidden her skin all these years. They followed the path back to the shore, noting the sections of flattened grass where Ebba had rested her bundle, the deep groove in the sand where she'd dragged it.

Even when they found Ebba's discarded clothes Myna couldn't bring herself to believe it. Not until she saw the two seals, not one, stop their play at her call and turn to look at her before deliberately swimming away, did the reality sink in.

'She's gone.'

At her words Ronan reached out and wrapped an arm around his wife.

'I should never have showed her where it was. I had no idea she could even use it.'

'Neither did I.' Myna forced a smile as she reached up to squeeze his hand.

'Are you all right?' he asked.

Myna squeezed her eyes shut, then opened them again. 'It's what children do, isn't it? Grow up, move out.' She tilted her face to kiss her husband. 'It's all right. It's as it should be.'

'Is it?' Ronan didn't seem so sure, but as the two bobbing heads disappeared in the distance Myna realised it was. She felt lighter than she had in years. No longer did the sea pull at her as it always had, no longer was she fighting the desire to dive in under the waves. Whatever Ebba had done when she had taken the skin, it had done one thing.

It had set Myna free.

About the Author

Heather Ewings is a Tasmanian author of speculative fiction. With a Masters in History and a fascination with myth and folklore, Heather's stories explore the past and the present (and occasionally the future) through the lens of the magical. Her short stories have been published both in Australia and internationally. Heather describes herself as a bookworm, a chocoholic, and a would-be hermit (if she didn't need to ferry her children to their myriad social events).

You can learn more about Heather and her stories, and sign up to her newsletter, at www.heatherewings.com.au.